Dangerous Curves Ahead

Ahead

— *Short Stories* —

Pat Ballard

Pearlsong Press
Nashville, TN

Pearlsong Press
P.O. Box 58065
Nashville, TN, 37205
www.pearlsong.com

ISBN: 0-9713247-2-7
Library of Congress Control Number: 2004102276
First Edition

Other books by Pat Ballard available from Pearlsong Press:

A Worthy Heir
His Brother's Child
Nobody's Perfect
Wanted: One Groom

*This book is dedicated to Jen Henderson
for all she's done to help people with weight-related issues.*

Contents

Dangerous Curves   7

Misconceptions   58

Freedom   68

The Clock   74

Playboy   84

The Promise of Winter   95

A Walk in the Park   102

The Company Party   109

A Weakness for Candy   113

Mail Order Bribe   117

Dangerous Curves

Damn! Damn! Damn! Sarah mentally screamed as she sat quickly on the ground, clutching the thumb she'd just smashed with the hammer.

"Are you okay, Mommy?" Aaron, her three-year-old son, hurried to her and slipped his small arms around her neck in an effort to comfort her.

"Mommy's okay. I just hit my thumb with the hammer," she tried to reassure him.

"I know. I heard it make a funny noise," he said. "Let me see," he added, reaching for her hand, great concern clouding his small face.

"No!" Sarah's eyes were still closed from the excruciating pain radiating from her thumb up to her elbow. "I'm okay. I just need a minute for it to quit hurting." She rocked back and forth with pain.

"Why did Daddy leave us? If he was here he could help you feel better." The sadness in the little boy's voice finished bringing the tears she'd been trying to hold back.

"He wanted to go somewhere else and live, but we'll be okay without him," she said weakly. How could she make her young son understand why his dad had left when she didn't even know the reason herself?

"Is he coming back?" She could tell he was close to tears, and knew he was upset because she was hurt. Any time he sensed she was upset, he started asking questions about his father. *Damn you, anyway, John Singley.* She silently cursed her ex-husband for putting her in the position she was in.

"Mommy?" Now Aaron was leaning over and whispering in Sarah's ear.

"Sweetheart, please just be quiet until Mommy's thumb stops hurting, then we'll talk more."

"Mommy!" He was closer and more persistent.

"What, honey?" No matter how badly she was hurting, she could never be impatient with him.

"Who's that man?" he asked in a low whisper.

Sarah's eyes flew open as a bolt of fear shot through her. She found herself looking into the eyes of a stranger.

At what point he had ridden up on the big sorrel horse, Sarah had no idea, but by the amused look on his face he had seen her hammer her thumb and had heard the exchange between her and Aaron. So he knew there was no man around.

"May I help you?" she asked, almost forgetting the pain.

"It looks like you're the one who needs help," he responded, without moving.

Sarah had never heard a voice like his—and yet, it was somehow familiar. It was so deep, she imagined she saw his chest vibrate when he spoke. She wondered how it would affect her if he were talking softly into her ear.

Dumbfounded at her own thoughts, she hastened to be rid of this stranger. "I'm okay. I really don't need any help. I don't think anyone's ever died of a smashed thumb."

"From the way it sounded when you hit it, it may be more than smashed. I think I should look at it, just to make sure." She watched in fascination as his tall frame unfolded from the saddle and stepped to the ground. He had to be at least six feet six inches tall, but handled his big frame with the grace and agility of a much smaller man.

He leaned over and said something to Aaron and the little boy went running toward their house.

Before she could ask what he'd said to Aaron, the man knelt beside her and took her hand in his. She was suddenly aware of her broken, unpolished fingernails. She'd been working outside all day, and looked as if she hadn't had a bath in a month. She was also aware of his large tanned fingers as they gently inspected her thumb.

"Ouch!" The exclamation ripped from her without warning.

"I think it's broken," he said, and looked up at her. The most beautiful blue eyes she had ever gazed into captured, held, and mesmerized her. Black wavy hair and tanned skin gave his eyes a surreal glow.

"Sarah? Are you okay? You aren't going to faint on me, are you? You don't look like the fainting kind."

Bringing herself back to reality, Sarah tried to smile. "No, I'm not going to faint. I'm okay. I'll go inside and put some ice on my thumb and it'll be fine."

"No. We've got to get you to the doctor. That thumb may need to be in a cast."

"NO!" Desperation caught at her throat. "I have too much to do around here before winter sets in! I *can't* have my thumb in a cast. A cast will only slow me down. Now please go away. I don't need you. I don't need anybody! Just go away!"

The day had been too much. She'd had to mend a fence on the far side of the property, and that took all morning. Then she'd barely gotten finished with lunch and put Aaron down for his nap, and sat down to try to figure out how she would pay some bills, when a storm had blown in and half ripped the barn door off. That's what she was trying to fix when she'd hammered her thumb.

She just wanted a shower and a soft bed to crawl into. She was so very tired.

"Here they are, Mister," she heard Aaron say, as he handed her truck keys to the stranger.

"Aaron Kyle Singley! What do you think you're doing?"

"I asked him to get the keys for me. I'm taking you to the doctor, so come on."

Without warning, Sarah felt strong hands under her arms, hoisting her to a standing position.

Her knees were still weak from the pain. They started to buckle slightly, causing him to put an arm around her for support. Again she was aware of how big he was. Not just tall. He was thick. Standing beside him now and looking at him, she wondered how the poor horse had held up under his weight. But she'd always wondered that about Matt Dillon's horse, too, when she used to watch Gunsmoke on TV.

He let go of her just long enough to loop his horse's bridle over a nearby fence post before leading her to the beat-up old pickup truck and helping her inside. Then, picking Aaron up, he walked around to the driver's side and got in, gently placing Aaron between them.

"Who are you? I shouldn't be getting into this vehicle with a total stranger." She was about to reach for the door handle when she felt his strong hand on her arm, detaining her.

"My name is Stewart Remington. I own the neighboring ranch to yours. I came over this afternoon to meet you, and had just ridden up when you hit your thumb."

Sarah was slightly appeased. She'd heard that a newcomer to the area had bought the Thompsons' ranch. As another wave of pain shot up her arm, she gave in and allowed him to drive her to the local hospital.

The next morning Sarah sat at her desk and looked unseeingly at the stack of bills waiting to be paid. Aaron was still asleep, and she knew she should take this time to do her paperwork, but she couldn't get her mind off the tall stranger who had ridden into her life yesterday afternoon.

Her thumb hadn't been broken, but the doctor told her not to use it for several days. Just another setback added to the string of bad luck she'd been having.

John had announced six months ago that he didn't love her anymore because she'd gotten fat after the baby was born. She'd been crushed that he would say something so hurtful, and tried to reason with him that the weight would probably drop off once her hormones settled back down after having the baby. But the little doubt in the back of her mind had reminded her that her mother was a plus-size woman and so was her grandmother. She knew she'd probably inherited their tendency to be larger than the tall, thin models that were so popular.

But John hadn't wanted to hear her reasoning. He wanted her to promise to lose the weight immediately or he would leave. When given an ultimatum and a time limit, Sarah's stubborn streak kicked in, and she'd told John to go ahead and leave. She'd suspected he was having an affair, anyway, and that he was just using her weight as an excuse to leave. Those suspicions were confirmed when he was married a month after their divorce became final.

What hurt Sarah the most was the fact that John had never asked to see Aaron since the divorce. He hadn't sent her any of the child support the court had ordered when they got the divorce, and she didn't have the time or the money to take him back to court.

He knew if things got bad enough she could sell the ranch and have money to live on. He'd always wanted to sell it, but the ranch had been in her family for three generations, and Sarah couldn't bear to part with it. Especially since it had been in her family for so long, and had meant so much to her ancestors. But now, not having John's second income to help defray the cost of running the ranch, she might have to sell after all.

He knew my name! The thought hit her like a bolt of lightning. Stewart Remington had called her Sarah yesterday when he'd knelt to check her thumb. She was sure she hadn't told him her name. Had he inquired from a neighbor? How did he know? A tiny thread of fear worked its way up Sarah's spine.

When they'd returned from the doctor's office and she and Aaron were inside for the night, Stewart had gone back out and finished repairing the broken barn door before he'd ridden away on his horse. At the time she'd felt grateful, and thought he was really going to be a good neighbor. But now she questioned his motives. Was he being a little *too* neighborly?

Stewart sat at his dining room table with the first cup of coffee of the morning. He reached into his wallet and took out a picture of Sarah and Aaron. Aaron was about two years old when the photo was taken, and Sarah had the look of a contented and happy mother. He'd thought from the photo that her eyes looked almost purple, but he wasn't prepared for their brilliance when he saw her with tears brimming in them. They were pure amethyst. And that hair! It was like spun gold. Very windblown. It was obvious she'd been working outside all day. *Probably the way it would look after making love*, he thought, smiling slightly.

And what a body! She had curves that could make a man drool. But he'd almost screwed up yesterday. He'd called her by name right up front. *Fool*, he chided himself. He couldn't afford for her to know who he was until the time was right. He had to be careful and not slip up anymore.

Sarah pulled the truck up to the curb and parked. She glanced around at the storefronts. Very little had changed in the small town of Langford as she grew up there, and she liked it like that. She wanted to raise Aaron in this small community, just the way she had grown up. And for that reason, she was prepared to do whatever it took to keep the ranch to pass on to him and his bloodline.

Last night she'd made up her mind to come into town this morning and talk with Hal Thompson, her banker, about getting a loan to help her along until she could find a way to make the ranch start supporting itself like it used to in the days before her father died. After he'd died her mother had tried to keep the ranch running, but with Sarah away at college her mother just didn't have the strength to manage a working ranch alone. Then her mother had died. Only a year after Sarah's father, but by then, the damage was done. When Sarah came home to take over the running of the ranch, the debts were so huge she had to sell off all the cattle just to keep the ranch. To make matters worse, when she and John were married he had no interest in trying to revive the production of the ranch.

But now, a new excitement gripped Sarah. She knew she retained enough knowledge from living and working on the ranch all of her life to make it work again. And she had the business degree she'd gotten in college, so she had all the tools to make this thing work. All the tools except money.

Taking a deep breath to build her confidence, she lifted Aaron from the truck. She was taking him into the bank with her. Part of her plan was to try to convince Hal Thompson, the president of the bank, that he needed to loan her the money to save her ranch so she could pass it on to little Aaron, here. She hoped the appeal would work.

Turning with Aaron in her arms, she found herself facing, and almost touching, Stewart Remington.

"Good morning." Again, Sarah was amazed at his voice. Every time he spoke, she could feel cold chills start to flit up and down her spine.

"Good morning," she answered, suddenly overcome with an attack of shyness, which was totally foreign to her.

"How's your thumb?"

"It's okay," she answered, feeling ridiculous. If she wasn't holding Aaron, she wondered if she would stick her finger in her mouth and start shuffling her feet in the sand like a silly schoolgirl. She had to snap out of this.

"Well, it's good to see you, but I was just headed for the bank," she said, desperate to break the awkward moment. "I'm going to try to get a loan to help me get back on my feet." *Shut up!* She silently admonished herself. He didn't need to know anything about her business. He was a stranger, for Pete's sake. And a suspicious stranger, at that.

"Can you have a cup of coffee with me first?" he asked, indicating the little RX drug store they were standing in front of. It was one of those rare small drug stores that still had a place to buy coffee, cold drinks, and even ice cream.

"Well—" Sarah started to hedge.

"Oh, come on. We won't stay long."

"Yeah, Mommy, Stoot wants to buy me a ice cream cone," Aaron pleaded.

"Aaron! You know not to ask people to buy you things. And you should say Mr. Remington."

"He told me to call him Stoot when you were at the doctor's." Aaron was having such a hard time saying Stewart, she could imagine what he would do with Mr. Remington.

"That's right, I did," Stewart said, reaching and taking Aaron from Sarah. "And, yes," he told the boy, "I would love to buy you an ice cream cone if it's okay with your mother."

The sight of Aaron being clutched so easily in the arms of the big man caught at Sarah's heart. Aaron needed a male figure in his life so badly. Surely a little time in the coffee shop couldn't hurt anything.

"Okay," she gave in reluctantly. "But just for a few minutes."

When they were settled at the little table with cups of coffee for Sarah and Stewart and an ice cream cone and glass of water for Aaron, Stewart kept Aaron on his lap and helped him with the ice cream, making sure the little boy licked in all the places that were trying to run down the cone. Aaron was losing the battle.

"Here, we'd better let your mom help you gain control of this," Stewart said, handing the cone to Sarah. And without thinking, Sarah took the cone and started gingerly licking all the places where the ice cream was melting and trying to run down the cone. She almost had the cone back under control when she looked up into the amused blue gleam of Stewart Remington's eyes. He was watching in fascination as she worked magic with her tongue on the ice cream cone.

Overcome with embarrassment, she quickly handed the cone back to Aaron. "Okay, I believe you can handle it now," she said, not looking at Stewart.

The chuckle that came from deep in his chest sounded more like a growl, and the chill that had threatened to run up her spine finally broke loose. She could feel goosebumps forming on her arms and knew without looking that her nipples were beading up in response to the chill. *Get a grip!* she commanded herself.

As hard as she tried not to, she felt compelled to look at Stewart. But his attention was drawn to the area where she felt the most distress. He was staring at her breasts in fascination.

Her first impulse was to reach up and cover her breasts with her hands. No one had ever made her this aware of her body. He looked at her as if he knew what she looked like without any clothes on.

Just then, Aaron gave a sharp indrawn breath as the ice cream plopped out of the cone and landed on the table in front of them.

"Mommy!" he yelped and started to cry.

"It's okay," she reassured him, and leaned over and scooped up the ice cream with her hand and put it back on the cone. "See? That was easy, wasn't it?" she said, and lovingly patted his cheek with the other hand, wanting to hug him for causing the distraction.

In the process of trying to wipe up the ice cream residue from the table her hand bumped Stewart's coffee cup. She jumped in reaction, and almost knocked the saltshaker off the small table. Stewart quickly reached to save the saltshaker, but instead his large hand wound up cupping one of her breasts. He quickly drew his hand back, but not before a charge of sexual need, like nothing she'd ever experienced before, shot through Sarah.

She had never in the entire five years of marriage with John been affected like this. She knew her breasts were rising and falling with her short gasps for air, as she and Stewart gazed at each other. She was captivated by those blue eyes, and felt as helpless as a bird caught in the hypnotic spell of a stalking cat.

"All done!" Aaron declared, and plopped his remaining ice cream cone into the glass of water, splashing cold water all over Sarah and Stewart, promptly breaking the spell.

Sarah hoped Stewart didn't notice her trembling hands as she hurriedly gathered Aaron and her purse and stood up.

"I really do have to get to the bank," she said, not looking at Stewart. Holding Aaron in her arms, she practically ran for the door.

Stewart watched Sarah's hips sway as she dashed toward the exit. She was all woman, and he couldn't wait to explore everything she had. He pulled a cell phone from his inside jacket pocket and dialed a number. "Hal, this is Stewart. Sarah Singley is headed for the bank to ask for a loan. Give her what she asks for. On second thought, find out what she wants the money for, and if she's not asking for enough, give her what you think she needs."

"You got it," the voice on the other end of the line answered, with no argument.

Sarah held her breath as she watched Hal Thompson go over the figures she'd given him. She had put everything that she needed, and why she needed it, in a written proposal before she left home this morning. She felt sure she'd done a good job in covering everything. Now if only he would lend her the money.

Finally, Hal looked up. He was a small man, just a little older than Sarah. She'd been three grades behind him in school, but she knew he'd always been a "brainy nerd," as the kids jokingly called him.

"You've done a good job in getting your facts together, but I don't see how $30,000 can cover what you really need to do," he said, taking his glasses off and looking at her.

Here it comes, she thought. *The rejection.* Now what would she do? She could feel the depression setting in.

"Why don't we start with $50,000, and if you need more, just say so," he said as casually as if he were asking her about the weather.

"What?" Sarah couldn't believe what he'd said.

"You want more?" Hal asked, looking up from the forms he'd started to fill out.

"No—I mean—" Sarah stuttered. "I was expecting you to turn me down totally, and here you are offering me more than I asked for. I'm just at a loss for words. I don't understand."

"Well," Hal said, taking his glasses off again, "I remember that ranch when it was very prosperous, and with the figures you've put on this paper, I think you can make it produce again. Plus, the boss told me to give you what I thought you needed to make the ranch work."

"The boss? I thought you were president of the bank."

"I'm the president, but not the owner. Stewart Remington owns the bank."

"Who is Stewart Remington?" she asked aloud, as the truck bumped its way up the dirt road that lead from the main highway up to her ranch.

"You know who Stoot is, Mommy," Aaron giggled in the seat next to her.

Sarah smiled at her son, but didn't comment. No, she didn't have the least bit of an idea who he was. She'd only met him yesterday, and yet she'd made a total fool of herself in the drug store today. How could that be? Sarah had always been a levelheaded, intelligent woman. Just about everything she'd done in her life up until this point had been rational and planned. Even as a teenager she'd never been boy-crazy, and John was the only person she'd ever really dated until she got married. Maybe she was just now going through her adolescence.

Well, she'd put a stop to this nonsense right now. She would make it a point to find out who Stewart Remington was, and she would make it a point to stop acting like a schoolgirl when he came around. Even better, she would just stay away from him. Far, far away. Then she wouldn't be in danger of making a fool of herself anymore.

Stewart sat in his office. A smile played around the corners of his mouth. If he'd been fascinated with Sarah Singley before today, he was captivated by her after this morning. He'd known she was a sensual woman, but this morning reaffirmed what he already knew. He would experience all she had to offer in due time.

Anticipation made his breathing harder, and a thrill ran through his lower body. What a body she had. Sure, she was larger than the women splashed all over the magazines, TV, and movie screens, and everyone to his own taste, but personally, he loved a woman with some curves. And, by damn, Sarah had some curves! Some *dangerous* curves! He couldn't wait to touch her all over. He knew how soft and willing she would be in his arms.

But he couldn't rush things. Oh, hell, he couldn't be around her and not rush things! Witness this morning. He felt like he'd known Sarah Singley for years. And now that she was this close, and he had seen her in person again, he couldn't stay away from her. He'd just have to be more careful and not frighten her away.

He reached for the phone and dialed. *Damn, the answering machine.*

"Sarah, give me a call when you get in." He left his number.

A thrill ran through Sarah as she listened to Stewart's message on the phone. Why did he want her to call him? Remembering her resolve just minutes before to stay away from him, she walked away from the phone. *But how are you going to find out who he is if you stay away from him?* a tiny voice questioned.

She argued back and forth with herself the whole time she was putting Aaron down for a nap.

When he was finally settled down and asleep, Sarah went to her office. She opened her books and entered the money she'd borrowed this morning. The figures looked so good sitting there on the ledger page. She leaned back in her chair and breathed a sigh of relief. A temporary sigh. She knew she had to prove her abilities, but at least now she had a chance to prove them. *You need to thank him, the little voice whispered.* "Oh, good grief!" she muttered, and reached for the phone.

"Who are you?" she asked, impulsively, as soon as Stewart had breathed a deep "hello" into the receiver.

"Pardon me?" he asked, just before he recognized Sarah's voice. "Sarah? What kind of question is that?"

"One that I need to know the answer to," she persisted.

"I'm a man who is very attracted to you and wants to come over to your house and bring dinner tonight."

His answer was the last thing Sarah expected.

It felt good to have a man say he was attracted to her. Her self-esteem had taken a beating when John had left, and she had convinced herself that *all* men wanted a size 6, model-type female on their arms, and nobody would want a larger woman like herself. Especially a hunk like Stewart Remington. Why was he trying to make her think he was attracted to her? Why had he acted like he did that morning? She didn't have anything he could possibly want. Her ranch was in the red, financially, and that's the only possession she had.

"Sarah? Are you still with me?" he asked in a teasing voice.

"Yes, I'm just trying to figure out your motive."

"My motive? What are you talking about?" The teasing note was gone now.

"Why are you coming on to me, and acting like you're attracted to a fat woman? As I said, Stewart, who are you and what do you want?"

Now the other end of the line was quiet for a long time. Finally, Stewart said, "Let me come over tonight, and I'll answer some of your questions."

"Okay," she gave in, reluctantly.

"I'll see you at six-thirty."

Sarah looked at herself in the mirror. She'd put on a snug fitting, slinky sky-blue dress that enhanced her eyes, and her curves. She had on more make-up than usual, and her nails were immaculate. She knew she was being silly, but it felt good to think that she might be just a little attractive to Stewart. She didn't consider herself a beautiful woman, but she surely wasn't the worst thing to look at. She'd caught men looking at her quite often, even after her weight gain. But she'd been so hurt over John's words and his leaving that she hadn't wanted anything to do with a man until Stewart came along.

Meaning? She stopped looking at her mirrored image and looked directly into her own soul.

"Mommy, Stoot's here," Aaron yelled from the living room before she could answer her own question.

Aaron had already let Stewart in by the time she made it to the living room. He looked stunning in black pants and a white western-cut shirt. He'd left the shirt open at the neck to expose a sprinkling of black chest hair trying to peek out. The long sleeves of his shirt were rolled up a couple of turns to reveal his strong, muscular forearms. He was, she decided on the spot, the most virile, sexual man she'd ever known.

"Hi," she breathed, already feeling his effect on her, and he was barely in the house.

"Hi, yourself," he answered. His eyes slowly roved over her body, seemingly an inch at a time, until she thought her lungs would burst from not breathing. Finally those electric blue eyes came back to hers.

"You look stunning," he said. Then added, "Absolutely beautiful!" And somehow, Sarah believed him. Maybe it was because she wanted to so badly, but she believed him.

She turned quickly away to help Aaron with what he was doing, so

Stewart couldn't see the tears that stung her eyelids. It had been so long since she'd felt beautiful. So long since anyone had told her that she was. In fact, John had never told her she was beautiful.

"Sarah." Stewart's hand was on her arm, turning her to face him. He thought he'd seen tears flash to her eyes when he told her she was beautiful. What kind of a son-of-a-bitch had John Singley been? And how badly had he hurt her?

When he looked deeply into Sarah's violet eyes, he saw the tears. But he also saw the flash of something else. A new hope. A new awareness of herself and what she had to offer a man. He saw the glimpse of the woman he knew was there.

"So, where's the dinner you promised?" she asked, trying to cover up her embarrassment.

"Oh, it'll be ready soon," he answered, with a mysterious look on his face.

"So what are you, a magician? You're just going to make it appear?" Sarah wondered what he was up to now.

"Something like that," he promised, just as a horn honked outside.

Sarah went to the door to see who could possibly be visiting. When she turned back to Stewart, her mouth was open with surprise. A big truck had pulled into the yard. She'd been so enthralled with her conversation with Stewart that she hadn't heard the noise. Several waiters scurried around on a flatbed trailer, setting up a table and chairs and spreading food on the table. In less than five minutes they were finished. They unhooked the trailer from the cab of the truck and drove away, leaving the trailer with a beautifully set table of wonderful-looking food. An umbrella shaded the table from the remaining rays of sunlight. Steps had been placed at the back of the trailer for easy access.

Stewart lifted Aaron up onto the trailer, then turned and offered Sarah his hand. She placed her hand in his and was amazed at how small it felt as his large fingers closed around it. He went up the steps first, leading her. His seating arrangement placed him at the head of the table with Sarah and Aaron on each side.

He placed food on Aaron's plate and set it down in front of the little boy.

"I don't like that," Aaron promptly replied, pointing to the broccoli casserole.

"What is it?" Stewart asked.

"I don't know," replied Aaron.

"Then how do you know you don't like it?" Sarah sat and watched as Stewart talked with Aaron as if he were his own son.

As Aaron shrugged his shoulders, Stewart said, "I'll make a deal with you. Take one bite and if you still don't like it you don't have to eat it, okay?"

"Can I spit it out if I don't like it?" Aaron asked.

"Aaron!" Sarah scolded.

"Now, wait, that's a fair question," Stewart said, trying to hide the smile on his face. "Yes, Aaron, you can spit it out if you don't like it. If you don't like it, just take it out of your mouth and put it right here on the side of your plate. That's what you do in a restaurant if you get something in your mouth that you don't like."

"Okay," Aaron agreed, and took a little dab of the broccoli casserole on his fork and put it in his mouth. He rolled it around on his tongue and tasted it, all the time watching Stewart closely. Then he took another slightly larger bite on his fork and did the same thing.

"You going to eat some?" he asked Stewart.

"You betcha!" Stewart answered.

"You going to eat some, Mommy?" he asked Sarah.

"Sure am," Sarah answered him, smiling.

"Okay, I'll eat it. It's not so bad." And he dug into the food on his plate as if he hadn't eaten in a week.

Sarah watched Stewart put food on her plate. Not only had he coaxed her son into eating something she'd never been able to get him to eat, he'd taught him a good-manners lesson in the act.

When Stewart had finished filling her plate, then his, he turned to her and caught her staring at him.

"Aren't you hungry? You haven't taken a bite yet. You can spit yours out too, if you don't like it," he assured her, with a teasing look in his eyes.

Taken off guard at his humor, Sarah laughed out loud. "I find myself being constantly amazed by you," she answered honestly.

"Good," he said. "I hope you continue being amazed by me." He added teasingly, "I have some really amazing things to show you later," and twitched his eyebrows at her. She laughed again, and Stewart found himself loving the sound of laughter bubbling up in her throat.

They sat for a few minutes in silence, enjoying the food and the atmosphere. Sarah was thinking how good it felt to have a man share a meal with her and Aaron again.

"Why would any man walk away from this?" Stewart asked unexpectedly, taking Sarah by surprise.

"He wanted to live somewhere else," Aaron answered, before Sarah had a chance to open her mouth.

"Then he must be a fool," Stewart whispered for Sarah's ears only, looking deeply into her eyes.

"What?" Aaron asked, feeling left out.

"Nothing," Sarah quickly told him.

"Why don't you come and live with us, Stoot? You could be my new daddy. And you could make Mommy feel better when she cries."

Stewart heard Sarah's sharply indrawn breath beside him, but he reached over and pulled the little boy to his lap.

"I'll make a deal with you, Aaron. I promise that I will always be very close, and the next time Mommy cries, you just tell me and I will do my best to make her feel better. Okay?"

"But wouldn't it be better if you lived with us?" he insisted.

"Aaron!" Sarah could take no more. She was about to go through the floor from embarrassment.

"Not yet," Stewart answered, and pulled the little boy's head down on his shoulder. He could tell the child was full and sleepy. He'd probably go to sleep in a few minutes if he'd sit still long enough.

Sarah sat and stared at the man holding her son. What had he just said? Not yet? "Not yet" to coming and living with them? Not *yet*? Did that mean he had intentions of trying to live with them? What was going on here? And she asked again, for the umpteenth time in the last two days, *who* is *Stewart Remington?*

Aaron was asleep in no time. Nothing could have looked more natural than the way Stewart sat holding her sleeping son. He looked as if he had been doing this kind of thing for years.

Stewart looked down at the sleeping child's cherubic face. "Why can't we stay this innocent forever?" he asked, knowing there was no answer.

"Who are you?" Sarah asked, reminding him that he had promised to tell her about himself.

"Where do you want me to start?" He knew he couldn't tell her everything. Not yet. But he could tell her enough to ease what questions she might have.

"Well, first, since I've never seen you before, how is it that you own the bank here in town?"

"Ahhh, Hal must have talked more that he should have, as usual."

"I've known Hal since I was a child. I don't find it unusual that he would tell me something like who owns the bank where he works," she defended.

"Do you remember Mamie Thompson?" His voice seemed to soften when he said the name.

"Yes. She was Tom Thompson's daughter. Mamie never got married. Rumor has it that she went away when she was a teenager and had an illegitimate child, but that was never proven. You bought the Thompson ranch, didn't you? So what about Mamie?"

"I am the illegitimate child."

Sarah could only stare at Stewart Remington, openmouthed.

"My father's parents raised me. My father disappeared after Mom—Mamie—told him she was pregnant, but his parents took Mamie in and took care of her until she had me. After I was born and she came back here, they raised me. I never saw my mother until several years ago. I found some pictures of her and my dad at my grandparents' home, and started asking questions. I started looking for my mom and dad. My grandparents were reluctant to tell me where she was for a while, but they finally did, and I came and found her. By then her father was dead, and her health was very bad. We got to know each other real well before she died. She left me everything she owned when she died. The bank was one of her many holdings. The ranch was another. I actually inherited the ranch. I didn't buy it."

"Did you ever find your dad? Do you mean he never came back to see his parents? How terrible!" Disbelief sounded in her voice.

"Yes, I found him. He had been killed in a car accident right after he left home. He didn't have any identification on him when he died. Only a picture of my mom. I kept a detective on the case until he found him. I think my grandparents were relieved that he was dead. That was easier to take than to believe he would just leave and never come home to see them."

"I can understand that."

Just then a clap of thunder sounded right over them. They had been so intent on their conversation that they hadn't noticed the approaching storm. Hurriedly, Stewart placed Aaron in Sarah's lap and lowered the umbrella and threw a heavy tarp over the remaining food and dishes. Then, taking Aaron in his arms, he and Sarah ran to the house. They barely made it to the front porch when the downpour hit.

Sarah led Stewart to Aaron's room, where he gently laid the little boy in his bed. He leaned over and lightly kissed his forehead before pulling the sheet up around his shoulders.

Sarah watched Stewart's actions with mixed emotions. She was in awe of this man who had come into her life, and how he seemed so taken with Aaron. But still a small warning voice kept asking why.

When Stewart stood and turned to her, she thought she saw the glimmer of tears in his eyes. Had he missed having a father so much?

Stewart took Sarah's arm and led her back to the living room. They stood for a moment at the window and watched the rain come down in torrents. The lightning flashed incessantly and the sharp cracking of thunder caused Sarah to shudder.

"Afraid of storms?" he asked, close to her.

"No, but I do have a healthy respect for them," she answered, realizing that if she leaned just the slightest, she would be touching him. Suddenly, she felt excitement growing inside her.

As if sensing what was going on inside Sarah, Stewart reached for her and pulled her to him. She didn't resist when he placed his hand under her chin and lifted her face to his. She watched, mesmerized, as his mouth lowered to claim hers. When his lips touched hers, they were cool and firm. She felt a tremor go through her, and she knew Stewart felt it too, because he drew her closer and deepened the kiss. She felt his tongue softly tracing the outline of her lips, and she parted them to give him access to her mouth. Someone groaned, but she wasn't sure which of them it was.

Her arms reached up to encircle his neck, and when they did, she felt his large hands slip to her waist and start a slow ascent upward. His hands slid up until they were almost to her armpits, then stopped. Then, slowly, they worked their way to each side of her swollen breasts. *Yes, yes*, she cried mentally, touch them, they need it so much.

As if hearing her, he started to unbutton the front of her dress. She could feel his fingers brushing her bare skin as each button responded to his strong fingers and opened up for him. Soon, she felt his hands slip inside her open dress, with free access to better feel what he was after. She gasped as he enclosed both mounds at once. But that wasn't good enough. She felt his hands slip to the back and start to unfasten her bra.

She was going to die from the mounting heat inside her. When she felt his hands grasp her naked flesh, she knew the moan she heard was her own voice. His lips left hers and went straight to his newfound treasures.

She cried out with delight at the things he was doing to her. He was making her feel things she had never felt with John—except that one magic night with him. How anyone could make love like John had that one time, but never again, was something Sarah could never understand.

She gasped as she felt Stewart's hand moving slowly down her stomach to grasp her most private spot. Then his mouth followed. He was kissing her, there, through her clothing. She had never even dreamed of anything like the shot of excitement that went through her when he gently took part of her between his teeth and bit down.

Slowly, through her dazed state of mind, Sarah became aware that Aaron was calling her. Stewart heard it, too, and abruptly stopped what he was doing.

"Mommy," the voice called again. Sarah started to go to him when Stewart's hand on her arm stopped her. Grinning, he pointed to her unbuttoned dress and exposed breast.

"I'll go," he said, while she hastened to put herself back together.

What had she almost *done*? Still dazed from her sexual arousal, she was horrified that she had been responding so readily to a man she had only known for two days. What was happening to her?

She was in the kitchen making a pot of coffee when Stewart returned.

"He's back asleep. It was just a dream," Stewart said, coming up behind her as she finished pouring water in the coffee pot.

"Is something wrong?" he asked, when Sarah didn't turn around to face him when her task was finished.

"How do you do it?" she asked, still standing with her back to him.

"Do what? Sarah, look at me. I don't want to talk to your back." Placing his hands on her shoulders, he turned her to face him. "Do what?" he repeated.

"You've been in our lives for only two days, and I find myself acting like a silly schoolgirl when you're around. And here you're able to go to my son's room and calm his bad dreams, and put him back to sleep with no trouble. And that's something his father could never do. How do you do it?" She shook her head in amazement as she gazed into his eyes. It seemed like she had known him forever.

"Didn't John make you act like a silly schoolgirl?" his voice was a low, husky growl.

"No—I mean—I—why are you asking me such a question anyway? What does that have to do with anything?" Sarah was frustrated that she had revealed more than she meant to. "Look, Stewart, you need to go. I'm really embarrassed about my actions. I need time to think." She played nervously with a dishtowel she had picked up from the counter top.

"Surely you're not serious! Listen to that storm. It may keep this up for hours if the storms we've been having are any indication. Let's just sit and talk, and have some coffee. I promise I'll be good." And he pulled out a chair and sat down at the table, as if to make his promise more believable.

But as he looked at Sarah, he couldn't help but lower his eyes to her breasts. Damn, they had been more beautiful than he had imagined. He could feel his arousal starting all over again, just thinking of her response to him.

"Stewart!" Sarah scolded, knowing where his thoughts were, because that's where hers were.

"I can't help myself, Sarah. You turn me on more than any

woman I've ever met. Hell, I can't even think straight when you're around. You make me feel like a schoolboy, too. All I can think of is touching you and making love to you." He spoke so earnestly that Sarah knew it wasn't just a line. She desperately wanted to believe he was telling the truth. If she didn't feel the same way, it might be harder to believe him.

"Come sit down and talk to me. Tell me about your marriage, and what went wrong. I want to hear all about you," he said, pulling out a chair beside him.

Instead of sitting close to him, Sarah went to the farthest end of the table and sat down.

A low, rumbling chuckle erupted from Stewart's chest. "Okay. That's probably the safest place anyway."

"I asked you first," Sarah insisted. "Why are my son and I responding to you like we are?"

"When something is right, it's just right. There doesn't always have to be a reason." Stewart knew this wasn't the answer Sarah was looking for, but it was all he could give her right now. "Now, your turn."

"John said he was leaving me because I was fat," Sarah stated bluntly. "He gave me an ultimatum on when and how much weight to lose, or he was leaving. I told him to start packing." She tried to hide the shame and hurt that came from telling this to a stranger. "I had suspected for a long time that he was having an affair, because he had basically stopped making—stopped having—" she realized she was about to tell a total stranger something very personal, and she couldn't bring herself to say it.

"Say it, Sarah," Stewart encouraged.

Sarah got up and poured two cups of coffee and brought them

back to the table. When she set Stewart's down in front of him, he caught her wrist. "Sit here, beside me. I'll be good. I've already promised."

She sat in the chair next to him, and took a sip of hot coffee. She knew he was waiting for her to resume her story, but she was suddenly overcome with shyness and couldn't look up from her cup.

"Sarah? I'm waiting."

She took a deep breath and looked deeply into Stewart's eyes. "John and I hadn't made love in over a year before he left. He'd said so many hurtful things to me about my size that I couldn't have responded to him even if he'd tried, which he didn't. I did try to lose the weight. And sometimes if I really starved myself, I would drop a few pounds, but when I would eat one solid meal, it would come right back on. He accused me of sneaking food when he was at work. He said anyone who wanted to lose weight could do it. I tried to point out to him that my mother and grandmother were both plus-size women, but he got angry and stormed out of the house. He didn't want to hear it.

"It really hurt me when he left, but the hurt was for Aaron. I know I'm better off without him. At least I don't have to wonder what he's going to say every time he walks in the house. I know men want their women to be tiny little things, but I just wasn't born to be a small person, so I guess I'll just have to live my life without a man, because I'm not willing to starve myself the rest of my life to be that size."

"Hey, back up, there. I just told you that you turned me on more than any woman I've ever known. Didn't you hear me? I think you're a beautiful size."

Sarah wished with all her heart she could believe him. Did a man like this really exist?

"Sarah, I'm taking back my promise. I'm not going to be good. I'm going to show you how much you turn me on, then maybe you'll believe me and stop talking this 'little woman' nonsense. You know, there are a lot of men that like a woman with 'a little meat on her bones', as the saying goes, and I happen to be one of them." He slid his chair closer to hers, and with one swift motion turned her chair to face him so she found herself positioned between his legs.

"What are you doing?" she shrieked, trying to back her chair away from him.

"I'm starting to be very bad," he answered, reaching for the top button of her dress.

"Stewart! No!" Sarah caught his big hand in hers and tried to stop him.

"Oh, Sarah, yes. I'm going to show you what you do to me." Even though Sarah clutched his hand in both of hers, trying to stop him, he slowly and deliberately undid each button, all the time gazing at what he was unveiling. When he had her dress unbuttoned to the waist, he slowly traced the outline of the top of her bra. The soft trickle of his fingers on her skin sent chills over her.

"You are a very sexy lady," Stewart growled, devouring the view before him. Then he took her hand in his and placed it on his arousal. "Feel what you do to me, Sarah. Would I be this hard if I didn't find you sexy? I want you so badly that I'm hurting. Can't you see that?"

Sarah's eyes were glued to the spot where her hand rested. It was very obvious that she affected him. It seemed she affected him *very much*.

"Do you believe me now? Or do you need more proof?"

"I believe you," she whispered.

"Do you want me too, Sarah? Are you suffering as much as I am?" He trailed his fingers down her arm until he had her hand in his grasp, then lifted it to his lips and kissed her palm. Sarah knew what her answer was, but she was afraid to say it out loud.

"Do you, Sarah?" Stewart persisted. "Do you want me to make love to you? You're going to have to tell me if you do, because I'm not going to force myself on you."

"Yes," her voice was barely audible.

"Yes, what?"

She was hypnotized by the blue gleam from his eyes.

"Yes, I want you to make love to me," she managed to say, in a voice that she didn't recognize.

"When? Tonight? Right now?" He continued to kiss her palm and caress the center with his tongue.

"Yes! Yes, right now!" she said, with conviction. He was driving her crazy. It had been so long since she had made love, she felt like a virgin again.

"Well, I'm not going to. Not tonight." And he started buttoning up her dress.

"What? What kind of game are you playing?" Now her voice was strong, and she could feel tears of shame start to burn the back of her eyelids. Again she'd let him make a fool of her.

"I'm not going to make love to you yet, because if I do, you'll wake up in the morning and hate both of us. You'll hate yourself for losing control, and you'll hate me for seducing you. So what I'm going to do tonight, is hold you all night long. I'm going to show you that all men aren't pigs, like your ex-husband. Will you let me do that, Sarah? Will you let me sleep in your bed and hold you until the sun wakes us up?"

Sarah couldn't believe what was happening. Was this a dream? She knew it wasn't a fantasy, because in her wildest fantasies, she could never have come up with something like this. Just the thought of what he was proposing to do was turning her on more than his lovemaking had.

"Well?" he questioned.

"And what if I say no? What will you do then?" The storm was still raging, and Sarah knew she couldn't send him out into a night like this.

"Unless you kick me out, I'll do it anyway."

She turned the coffee pot and kitchen light off, and then held her hand out to Stewart. Trembling with the knowledge of what she was about to do, she led him to the bedroom where she'd spent so many miserable nights with John.

The lightning was as continuous as strobe lights. Even with all the lights in the house off, she could still see Stewart clearly. Once they got inside the room, she didn't know what to do next, but she didn't have to wait. Stewart took the lead again and led her to the side of the bed, where he very slowly and gently undressed her. His eyes never left her body as he visually explored each portion he uncovered. When all her clothes lay puddled on the floor around her feet, he turned the covers back and motioned for her to lie down. Then he stood, while she watched, and pulled off his own clothes.

She was amazed at his body. He was even more strong and powerful looking in the nude than with his clothes on. When he had finished undressing, he got into bed beside her, and wrapped his arm around her waist.

"Do you like to watch the storms at night?" His breath fanned her hair, close to her ear.

"If they aren't really bad," she answered. "If they're really bad, I put my head under the covers so I can't see."

"Just like a kid," he accused, as he positioned himself closer to her. She lay on her back, and he was on his side facing her. Now, the length of his body lay against her. She could feel his arousal pressed against her side. She couldn't imagine getting any sleep tonight.

She reached down to pull the cover up around her neck, but he stopped her.

"I like the view in the lightning," he chuckled.

Looking down, she was made keenly aware of her exposed breasts standing proud, with Stewart's arm resting across her body, just under them.

Desire caused her lower body to pulsate. She didn't want him to just lie here and talk. She wanted him to make love to her. She wanted to make love to him.

"Stewart," she pleaded.

"Shhhhhh. We can do this. It's going to be extremely difficult, but we *can* do this. Tell me about John. What was he like? Did he love you?"

Reluctantly, she gave in and started talking. "In looking back over our marriage, I don't believe John ever loved me. I think now that he just married me because he knew I had this ranch, and thought he could persuade me to sell it so he could wind up with a lot of money. When he finally realized I had no intentions of selling, he started pulling away from me. Soon after that, I started suspecting he was having an affair. He started staying out later and later at night, and sometimes he didn't come home at all."

"Did you love him?"

"When we first met, and started dating, I thought I did. But now, I think I just went for him because he was new to this area. Someone different from the boys I had grown up with. He was just out of college and he seemed so intelligent. I guess I was a little flattered that he picked me out of all the other girls around. Ha! What a joke," she ended bitterly.

"Did you enjoy his lovemaking?" Stewart wondered if she would answer, but after a brief pause, she did.

"No." The answer was blunt. Then, chuckling embarrassedly, she continued. "John didn't even attempt to make love. He just basically took what he wanted, and that was about it." She hesitated for a moment, then added, "Except for that one time."

Did she imagine it, or did Stewart quickly suck his breath in?

"What do you mean?" He hoped his voice sounded normal as he asked the question.

"We'd gone into town to a big party and street dance. I'd had way too much wine to drink, so I went back to our hotel room before John did. I had been asleep, but when he came in, I woke up. I was still affected by the wine, and wine makes me very amorous, so I wanted to make love. He didn't want to at first. Normally, I would have just turned over and cried, but with all that wine in me, I refused to give up. And, wow! He was good that night! In fact, I'm pretty sure that was the night I got pregnant with Aaron. We made love all night." She breathed in a long sigh. "I could never get him to even talk about it, much less make love to me like that, again. But at least I got Aaron from it."

"Why do you believe you got pregnant that night?" Stewart's husky voice was barely above a whisper.

"Because I never had another period after that until Aaron was born, and I'm pretty sure we didn't have sex again soon enough to have allowed Aaron to be born when he was. Anyway, this has to be boring to you. Tell me about your childhood." She realized that talking did keep her mind off of the man lying beside her to some degree.

Not long after Stewart started telling a deliberately boring story from his childhood, he heard Sarah's breathing become rhythmic and knew she was asleep.

Stewart Remington got little sleep that night. But he didn't mind. He spent the night planning the future.

When Sarah awoke, she became aware of the sun beaming in through her bedroom window, and the sound of running water. She leaped from the bed, about to check on Aaron, when the clump of men's clothing lying on the floor reminded her of the night before. The running water was Stewart taking a shower.

She was about to go into Aaron's room and check on him when she noticed that Stewart's wallet had fallen out of his pocket and lay beside his pants. Did she dare look inside? That might give her some answers. At least, she could find out if Stewart Remington was his real name.

Keeping her ears tuned to the running water, she reached down and picked up the wallet. Feeling guilty for intruding on someone's personal property, she slowly opened the wallet. There gazing back at her was a photo of her and Aaron. A photo that she'd had taken about a year ago. The photo that John had carried in his pocket ever since she'd had it made! A cold hard fear settled over Sarah.

Hearing the water shut off, she quickly placed the wallet exactly where she'd found it and jumped back under the bedcovers. Trying to look as normal as possible, she waited for Stewart to come back to the room.

She heard him come in, but pretended to be asleep until she felt him sit down on the bed beside her. She opened her eyes slowly, hoping it looked like her first waking of the morning.

"Good morning, sleepyhead," he said, pushing the sheet down from her chin.

"Hi," she responded, trying to give him a normal smile.

"I've made coffee, and I really wish I could stay and make breakfast for you, but I'm running late for an appointment this morning, so I have to go. I'll call you later." And he leaned down and placed a gentle kiss on her sleep-swollen lips.

Sarah sat at the dining room table, clutching the hot cup of coffee in her shaking hands. She was sitting in the very chair where she sat last night and virtually begged a stranger to make love to her. The same stranger that all the while had a photo of her and her child in his wallet. A photo that used to be in her husband's pocket! She felt the hair on the back of her neck prickle with the fear that chorused through her body. She had to get a grip. Had to figure out how to attack this mystery.

Who was Stewart Remington? What did he want? And why did he have a photo of her and Aaron in his wallet? Was that story about being Mamie Thompson's son just a line?

A thought flashed across her mind, and she ran to the phone and dialed information for the deeds office at the courthouse. After asking a few questions, the voice on the other end assured her that Mamie Thompson had left all her holdings to a Mr. Stewart Remington.

Sarah felt a little better when she hung up the phone. At least that part of his story was true.

Surely John would know how Stewart came to have the photo. She dialed his number.

"Hello, Singley's Engineering," a young female voice answered.

"John Singley, please," Sarah requested.

"Who's calling?"

"Sarah," she answered shortly.

"Sarah who?" Sarah declared she could hear gum smacking.

"Oh, for Pete's sake, tell him his ex-wife is on the phone!" she demanded impatiently.

"Oh, we can't take any calls from you. Mr. Singley said absolutely no calls from you."

"Look, this is an emergency. You get John Singley on the phone now!" Sarah heard an indignant grunt as the phone went silent. She thought she had been hung up on until she heard the piped music in the background.

"Sarah, this better be good." John wasn't even trying to hide his irritation.

"John, why does Stewart Remington have the picture of Aaron and me that you used to carry in your wallet?"

"Well, it was the weirdest thing." The irritation had left John's voice now that he knew she wasn't going to ask for anything. "I was at a bar one night having a drink before I came home, like I always did, and this big dude was sitting beside me. When I opened my wallet to pay, that picture fell out, and the guy asked if he could have it. So I gave it to him."

"Didn't you think that was a little strange?" she asked, wondering how she had put up with the man for as long as she had.

"Oh, hell, Sarah, I was half drunk when it happened. Yeah, now, thinking about it, it seems damn strange. So how'd you find out he had it? Is he there?" Something like suspicion edged his voice.

"John, do you know this man? Who is he?" She hedged answering his questions.

"I met him once, a long time ago." Now John's voice sounded secretive.

"When? Where? I need to know."

"He was there in Langford several years ago. Something about visiting his sick mother or something. I didn't get to know him, just met him at a party one night. Look, Sarah, I gotta go, I'm running late for a meeting. See ya." And the phone went dead in Sarah's ear.

Sarah stared at the phone. Her brain hurt from trying to figure this out. And her conversation with John sure hadn't helped any. Why would Stewart want a picture of her and Aaron? If anything, her conversation with John left her with more questions.

The shrill ringing of the phone startled her back to reality.

"Hello?" she said quickly, hoping it was John calling back with added information.

"Sarah? Are you okay? You sound strange." The deep voice on the other end of the line was not what Sarah wanted to hear.

"Yes, I'm okay." She tried to sound normal.

"Listen, I just got a call, and I have to be out of town for a week or two. I'll call you and give you my phone number when I know what hotel I'll be staying in. That way, if you need anything you can let me know. I'll talk with you tonight, okay?"

"Okay," was all Sarah could manage to say. Here was a man acting more concerned about her welfare after two days than John had ever acted in their entire marriage. Also, this man had a photo of her and her child, and apparently had carried it for many months. So technically, he had known her longer than she had known him, even if it was just from a photo.

Or was it just from a photo? She'd heard about stalkers. Had Stewart been stalking her? Again, fear threatened to take over her common sense.

Stewart settled back in the plane seat. *Damn!* He didn't need to be away now. He felt like he was making such good progress with Sarah. In just two days, too. He grinned. Well, when something's right, it's just right. That had always been his motto.

He mentally went over the night before. It had taken every ounce of his self-control not to make love to her. He'd thought it would get better after she went to sleep, but it was only worse, because he had the freedom to watch her as he pleased, as she lay sleeping. He could feel his arousal starting again, just remembering how beautiful she was, lying there with her breasts exposed as she softly breathed. He'd finally had to turn his back to her and try to concentrate on something else.

He'd listened to little Aaron's soft breathing. Once, when he'd cried out in his sleep, Stewart had eased out of bed and gone in to comfort the sleeping child. Aaron was back sound asleep by the time Stewart reached his bed, but Stewart had sat down and patted him gently, stayed by his side for a long time, just watching him sleep.

Stewart Remington had felt complete last night, for the first time in his life.

As the plane soared through the skies, he leaned his head back and caught up on some of the sleep he'd missed the night before.

Sarah spent the next week trying to keep her mind off of Stewart Remington. As he promised, he called every night to check on her and Aaron. During each day she would tell herself how weird the situation was, and promise herself that she would question him more closely when he called that night, but as soon as she heard that deep voice on the other end of the line she became captivated, and even when she did ask him a question, his answers were so valid she had to believe him.

At the sound of a vehicle approaching, Sarah looked up from the bookwork she was trying to get finished. From the sound of the motor, it was a big vehicle. She went to the front door just in time to see a huge cattle truck pull up to her barn and stop. A man jumped out of the passenger's side and went to the back of the trailer.

"Hey! Wait!" she yelled, running down the steps, trying to stop them before they unloaded the animals.

"Mrs. Remington?" The driver came around the truck and met her. He had a clipboard in his hand.

"No! My name is Sarah Singley. I'm not Mrs. Remington. You're at the wrong place. I think you want to go to the neighboring ranch," she explained.

"No. I have explicit directions to bring these cows to this location. See?" And he held the directions out for her to read.

"But I haven't ordered any cows. I've been shopping, and making some calls, but I haven't ordered any yet. It had to have been Stewart Remington, because you thought I was his wife. This isn't his ranch. He owns the Thompson ranch now. So take the cows over there."

"Ma'am—my orders are to leave these cows here. Now you can show me where you want 'em, or I can just let 'em go right here in your yard. I don't aim to sound hard-nosed about this, but I ain't got all day to try to figure out an alternate plan, when my instructions are real clear. I got other loads to haul, and I can't make no money standing around trying to second guess my instructions."

Sarah could tell he would make good his threat to set the cows free in her yard, so she opened the gate to her main pasture. Soon there were 20 choice breeding cows and a fine specimen of a bull grazing happily in her pasture. It wouldn't hurt for them to stay there until Stewart got home. Then he could see that they got to his ranch.

That night he called at seven o'clock, as usual.

"Stewart, some guy brought a truckload of cows this morning," she hastened to tell him.

"Do they look good?" he asked, not at all surprised.

"Yes, they're choice stock, but the truck driver brought them here, instead of to your place. I let him leave the cows here, since he had directions to my ranch instead of yours for some reason."

"But they're yours," Stewart said reasonably from the other end of the line.

"No they aren't. I haven't purchased any cows yet."

"But you said on the phone the other night that you had found some cattle you were fairly sure you were going to get. I know the rancher who handles those cows and I know they're great stock, no diseases or problems, so I called him and had them sent to you. Is 20 head enough to start on? And how's that bull? His name's Tom-Tom, and the previous owner said he turns out some fine looking calves."

"I don't understand. Why are you doing all this?" She was at a loss for words.

"I'm doing it to help you. We can settle up money-wise when I get home. Now, if you aren't satisfied with the cows, I'll take them for myself when I get back. I know they're some of the best that money can buy and I'll be glad to keep them. Did I overstep my boundaries by sending them? I meant to call and let you know they were coming, but I've been tied up in meetings all day. I'm sorry. I'll get better at this, I promise."

"Mommy, is that Stoot? Let me talk! Let me talk!" Aaron had heard her on the phone. And as usual, Stewart spent a few minutes asking Aaron about his day. *Just like a real dad.* Sarah couldn't keep the comparison from entering her mind.

What had he meant, "he'd get better at this?" He sounded like he was planning for a long-term relationship. Sarah felt like she was losing her mind. She couldn't think of anything except Stewart Remington. Half the time she was remembering his lovemaking, and how it affected her, and the other half of the time she was trying to figure out if he was a stalker. What if she was involved with a serial killer or something horrible like that?

She turned and tossed all night, with strange dreams of someone chasing her to do her harm. But when he caught her, he made sweet, passionate love to her. She woke up dreaming that she and John had made love all night like they did that one time, but it wasn't John she had dreamed about, it was Stewart.

She finally gave up on trying to sleep and went to the kitchen and made coffee.

As soon as she knew the bank was open the next morning, she called Hal Thompson.

"Hal," she asked as soon as he answered, "how well do you know Stewart Remington?"

"Well, I've worked pretty closely with him since he inherited all of the Thompsons' holdings, which was quite a substantial amount. Not only money, but also this bank and several stores here in Langford. He's a shrewd businessman, but he seems to go out of his way to be fair to everyone he deals with. I understand he has quite a reputation in the business world. Does that answer your question?"

"Well, not really, but I guess it helps a little. And, Hal, if for some reason you talk with Stewart, don't tell him about this conversation, please." Sarah didn't want Stewart knowing she was checking up on him. That might make him suspicious if he really was up to something.

As soon as Sarah hung up the phone, Hal Thompson dialed Stewart's cell phone.

"Stewart," he answered.

"She called. She's asking about you. Stewart, you're going to have to come clean with her soon."

"I know. I'm not sure, but I think she may have seen the picture. She's acting a little different. Man, I really appreciate you calling me."

"That's okay, Cuz."

Stewart put the phone back in his pocket. Hal was a good man. They'd been instant friends as soon as they found out they were actually cousins. Hal's grandmother had been Tom Thompson's sister. Hal had grown up as an only child, like Stewart, and when they found that they were cousins it was almost like finding a long-lost brother. Hal had been a great help in making Stewart's plan come together.

As the plane took off, Stewart leaned back in his seat again and smiled. He was going home. What a good feeling that was. He'd finally found a place that felt like home to him. His grandparents had been good to him and had given him a good life, but he'd always had the feeling that he was intruding on them. Kind of like they didn't really want him there, but didn't have a choice. But now it was different. He felt like he belonged in Langford. And he knew that in time Sarah would come to love him as much as he loved her. She just had to. He'd find a way to make it happen.

Sarah finished cleaning the dinner dishes and sat down with a magazine to wait for the phone to ring. If Stewart called tonight at seven o'clock, as usual, she was just going to come right out and ask him about the picture. She'd tried to think of a way to find out why he had the photo, but she couldn't come up with any ideas. But one thing was for sure—she wasn't going to live her life in fear. She would get to the bottom of this, and the sooner the better.

She just couldn't believe Stewart was a stalker, though. In a town as small as Langford, someone would have noticed a stranger skulking around, and surely would have mentioned it to her. But on the other hand, he'd managed to acquire half the town, plus move in and become established on the Thompsons' ranch, without her knowing it.

The ringing of the phone caused her to look at the clock. Right on time.

"Hello," she said into the receiver.

"You have a beautiful voice. Have I ever told you that?" Stewart said, without any preliminaries.

"No, but thank you," she answered, all her fears dissipating as soon as she heard his voice. Just like the days and nights of the past week. She would spend her days conjuring up all kinds of motives that Stewart might have, then as soon as she heard his voice, everything vanished except the way he made her feel.

"I'm home. And so glad to be here." She noticed the weariness in his voice. "I want to take you to dinner tomorrow night. Can you make it?"

"Yes. I don't have a lot of evening plans, as I'm sure you are aware." A hint of sarcasm crept into her voice.

"Well, I plan to change that situation, for sure. I plan to fill up your evenings." The soft promise in his voice started the chills up Sarah's spine. If she lived with this man for a thousand years, she would never get tired of his voice. Whoa! Where did that thought come from? Live with him? She raked her fingers through her hair, trying to gain control of her pounding heart.

"Sarah? You still there?"

"I'm here." She hoped he didn't notice the breathless catch in her voice.

"Is it okay if we get a babysitter tomorrow night? I'll pay for someone to come and stay with Aaron if you know of anyone."

"I use one of the neighbors' teenage daughters when I need someone. I can usually get her on fairly short notice." They talked for a few more minutes before they hung up.

Stewart stared at the phone several minutes after hanging up. Well, this was it. He'd wanted to wait a little longer and let Sarah get to know him better, but things had progressed faster than he could ever have dreamed. He knew he found her extremely attractive, but he'd had no idea that the sexual tension would run so high between them. Even on the phone, he could tell Sarah was as affected as he was. He loved the way her breath caught in her throat when she was talking sometimes. He wished he knew which thoughts she was having that caused her breathing to go all short and sexy.

Hopefully, if everything went okay, tomorrow night after an expensive bottle of wine, he might find out. It all depended on how she was going to react to that other thing—

Sarah's hands shook so badly she could hardly get dressed. Everything had gone perfectly, so far. Janet was able to come over and stay with Aaron. She'd been able to get into town and have the hairdresser put her hair up in a beautiful sweep on top of her head. And she'd even bought a new dress. She knew she shouldn't splurge on her hair and a dress, but it had been so long since she'd been out, she felt she deserved to give herself a special treat.

Excitement mingled with just a touch of apprehension as she applied the finishing touches of her makeup. She wouldn't let herself think about what the night held, but she knew one thing for sure, she would get to the bottom of the Stewart Remington mystery before the night was over.

She barely recognized herself as she gazed at her reflection in the mirror. Soft golden tendrils formed a halo around her face, and the purple chiffon dress made her eyes look like huge pools of liquid amethyst. The mid-calf-length dress flowed with each step she took, making her feel like a princess. A soft glow of anticipation emanated from her face.

She was giving Janet some final instructions when she heard the knock on the door.

Sarah felt the breath leave her body as she gazed at Stewart. She wasn't prepared for the way he looked in an expensive navy suit, with a tie that exactly matched the blue of his eyes. She knew she had to breathe or she was going to pass out.

Stewart was having the same reaction to her. They stood for what seemed like an eternity and gazed at each other, neither being able to speak.

"Stoot! Stoot! You came home!" Aaron squealed in delight,

running to greet him and once again breaking the spell.

Stewart swooped Aaron off his feet and swung him high in the air. He seemed as happy to see Aaron as Aaron was to see him. Sarah marveled at the connection between this man and her son.

"Hiya, sport! I brought you something." Standing Aaron down, Stewart reached over to one side of the door where he had hidden the surprise and handed Aaron a sack of "goodies."

"Wow!" shouted the little boy. He immediately sat down on the floor and started pulling out toys.

"And now," Stewart said, turning to Sarah, "may I have the honor of escorting the most beautiful woman in the world to dinner?"

"Why, Suh, Ah would be honahed," Sarah answered in her most southern accent.

Dinner was finished, and Sarah couldn't believe how much she had enjoyed herself. John would never talk *with* her. He always talked *at* her, as if he felt he had to be her constant tutor. But she and Stewart had discussed everything from politics to raising children. He had listened to her point of view and had agreed on most, but even when he didn't agree, he was always quick to point out that it was just "his opinion."

She leaned back in her chair, holding her third glass of wine. She needed to be careful and not drink too much, but she needed the extra courage to ask the questions she had to ask. Because, even though she'd had a wonderful evening, she was still determined to find out why this captivating man carried a photo of her and her child in his wallet.

"Sarah," Stewart interrupted her thoughts. "Will you come back to my house for a few minutes when we leave here? I'd like for you to see where I live."

Sarah lifted her eyebrows at what sounded like a typical line.

Laughter erupted from Stewart. "No, honestly, I want you to see my home. I promise not to take advantage of you. Not until you ask me to, that is," he added with an extra twinkle in his eyes.

Sarah blushed, remembering how she had practically begged him to make love to her.

As a child, Sarah had always loved the Spanish-style design of the Thompsons' home, but had never been inside the house. Now, as Stewart opened the door and led her inside, she was equally as impressed. The bottom floor was totally open, obviously meant for entertaining and family gatherings.

As they made their way into the interior, Sarah noticed a huge stone fireplace at the far end of the room. She moved closer so she could see it better—and stopped cold in her tracks.

The breath lodged in her throat as she stared at a life-size portrait of Aaron hanging over the antique wooden mantle. A portrait of Aaron that she had never seen.

Suddenly all the fears and apprehensions she'd had for the past two weeks culminated in a lump in her throat. For what seemed like an eternity she stared at the portrait, but couldn't speak. She was aware that Stewart was standing beside her, watching her.

Finally, taking a deep, ragged breath, she asked, "What—are—you—doing—with— a—portrait—of—my—son?"

Sarah's whole body was shaking from the reaction of seeing Aaron's portrait hanging over a stranger's fireplace. It confirmed her fears. Something was drastically wrong with this situation.

"Come, sit on the sofa with me, and I'll explain," Stewart said, putting his arm around her to help support her. He led her to the sofa.

He took a photo album from the coffee table and placed it across their laps. When he opened it, it was full of pictures of Aaron with strangers. Sarah raised horror-stricken eyes to Stewart's face. How? When had these pictures been taken? She felt as if she were in the twilight zone.

"Sarah, these pictures aren't of Aaron. They're photos of me when I was his age. I brought you here tonight to show these to you. It's time you knew the truth." Stewart had his arm around her shoulders as he spoke, and he held her hand in his.

She sprang from the couch and turned on Stewart. "What do you mean, they're you? How could this be? Please just tell me what's going on! Tell me!" she screamed. "What's going on? And why do you have a picture of Aaron and me in your wallet?" She'd almost forgotten about that photo.

"Come sit down, Sarah, and I'll explain," Stewart coaxed. He knew this was going to be hard on her, but the hardest part was yet to come.

"NO! I don't want to sit down. Just talk to me!" she demanded, glaring at Stewart as if she would physically attack him at any minute.

"Sarah, remember that night you said John and you made love all night?"

"Yes, but what does that have to do with what we're talking about right now?"

"That was me, not John. Sarah, Aaron is my son." The gentleness in his voice couldn't ease the shock of his words.

"*What?*" Sarah's stunned voice uttered, as she sank to the floor in front of him. "But how? That's not possible."

"That night, you'd had way too much wine to drink. I know because I had watched you all night at the party. I couldn't keep my eyes off of you. I thought you were the most beautiful woman I'd ever seen. As I watched you, you were watching your husband flirt with a redhead at your table. The hurt in your eyes broke my heart, and I wanted to hold you in my arms and comfort you. You endured his actions as long as you could, but finally left.

"John really went after the redhead when you were out of sight. Finally, I couldn't stand it any longer, so I went over to him and told him if he was any kind of man at all, he would go find you and comfort you. Well, the bastard took his hotel key out of his pocket and handed it to me and told *me* to go comfort you.

"I knew I was making a mistake going to your room, but I told myself that I would just go and make sure you were okay, then I would leave. I knocked several times on the door, but when you didn't answer, I really did get concerned, and let myself in. It was dark in the room, but I found you in the bed asleep and was about to leave, knowing you were okay, when you woke up and thought I was John.

"When you started to initiate the lovemaking, I tried to stop you, but you kept trying to seduce me, and I'd had a couple too many myself, so I gave in and made love to you. Sarah, I've never done anything like that in my life, but you were the sexiest woman I had ever had in my arms, and I realized just once wasn't enough. I had to have you over and over, because I didn't think I would ever see you again. The next morning I left before you woke up, but walking out of that room was the hardest thing I'd ever done."

"I always knew I got pregnant that night," Sarah whispered. She was relaxing a little now, finally understanding some of the puzzle. But how could John have stooped so low?

As if reading her mind, Stewart continued, "About a year ago,

John contacted me. He knew that Aaron was mine, because he knew he couldn't father a child. Did he ever tell you that?"

"No!" Sarah said with more disbelief in her voice.

"He was wounded as a child, and knew he would never be a father. When he found out that I had come into quite a bit of money, he contacted me and said that Aaron was mine, and tried to blackmail me into giving him money to help raise Aaron."

Sarah covered her face with her hands. Shame for her ex-husband flooded her.

"I made arrangements for John to bring Aaron into town for a blood test. But as soon as I saw him, I knew he was mine. I didn't need a blood test. I insisted that John give me the photo that was in his wallet so I could take it home with me and compare it with my childhood pictures.

"I was elated when I heard you and John had divorced. I knew I would finally be able to pursue my love for you."

"Your love for me?"

"Yes. You see, after that magic night with you, I couldn't get you out of my mind. No other woman has ever come close to satisfying me like you did. Sarah, I want more than anything to marry you and make a home for you and Aaron. I know that this is sudden for you, but I do believe you feel something for me, don't you? Do I have a chance?"

Up until two weeks ago, Sarah had never believed in love at first sight, but now she knew better. Actually, though, she had loved Stewart for almost four years. She had loved him ever since that magic night they'd spent together. Somehow, she had known all along that John wasn't in her bed that night. She'd always wondered why she couldn't get him to talk about it with her. Now she knew.

"Sarah?" His voice implored. "Will you give me a chance?"

"Yes, Stewart, I'll give you a chance," she said. "Starting right now."

And she reached up to kiss him.

Misconceptions

Lila watched the "up" arrow as she listened to the approaching elevator. As it clunked to a stop and the doors slid open, she smelled expensive men's cologne before she spotted the man in a dark gray suit in the far corner.

"Good morning," she murmured, stepping inside and reaching automatically for the fifth floor button. But it was already lit.

She jerked to instant alert. He was going to the same floor as she. Could this be—?

She glanced cautiously over at him and was startled to find him blatantly staring at her. Giving him a small, polite smile, she lowered her eyes from his intent gaze.

Was this the new manager who was supposed to arrive at Fessler's Group today? If this was the new manager, she knew a group of women who were going to be extremely excited. He was gorgeous! Dark hair, maybe even black, styled to a "T," and eyes that looked like blue crystal. There were going to be some catfights, unless, of course, he was married. A smile played around the corners of Lila's mouth as she predicted the future of the office where she worked.

The elevator stopped and she headed for her office without looking back to see where the handsome stranger headed. If he was the new manager, she'd hear about it soon enough.

In less than ten minutes Charlotte, Lila's best friend and co-worker, slid conspicuously into Lila's office.

"Guess who's here," she whispered, as if someone could hear through the walls.

"The new manager?" Lila whispered back.

"How did you know? I thought I was going to be the first to tell you. Darn!" Charlotte loved office gossip, and kept Lila more informed than she would rather have been.

"Is he tall, dark and handsome?" Lila asked, smiling mischievously at her friend.

"Oh, yes. But more like tall, dark, and breathtakingly, stunningly, gorgeous! But how did you know? Surely, you haven't met him already."

"I rode up in the elevator with him." Lila deliberately looked smug.

"You lucky dog! Did you talk to him?"

"Nope. We made passionate love, but we didn't say a word."

"Oh, stop poking fun at me! I know you don't get as excited about new men on the scene as I do, but you've got to admit, he's really something else!"

"Yes, and you've got to remember that, as always, when new management arrives, heads roll. Don't get too excited about this new man until you know if he's married, or if any of us still have a job after he's been here a few weeks." Lila hated to spoil Charlotte's mood, but her friend didn't always do very good reality checks.

"Yeah, like you're worried. You're the secretary to the top dog around here. You're not going anywhere," Charlotte said. She added solemnly, "I, on the other hand, may have a problem." Charlotte's attendance wasn't as good as it could be, and she had been warned on several occasions that she needed to shape up.

"Oh, come on now, I didn't mean to throw a cloud over your good mood. You're going to be fine. Beautiful, shapely blondes like you seldom have to worry about their jobs when a man is the boss." A touch of cynicism crept into Lila's voice.

Before Charlotte could comment, the intercom on the phone system interrupted to call everyone to a meeting in the conference room. Lila and Charlotte were some of the early arrivals, so they sat fairly close to the head of the huge oval conference table.

Mr. Hoffman, the president of the company, stood and introduced the new manager, Ted Carmike.

Lila listened carefully as Ted Carmike gave his "this is who I am, and this is what I want to accomplish" speech. Everything he said sounded wonderfully progressive, but Lila knew they were experiencing the lull before the storm. As he finished and started to sit down, Charlotte asked, "Are you married?" Laughter and several "good question" comments came from female voices around the table.

"No, I'm not married," Ted Carmike said, looking directly into Lila's eyes.

"I didn't ask the question!" Lila said quickly, but applause from surrounding co-workers drowned her out.

With the meeting drawing to a close, Mr. Hoffman stood up and reminded everyone about the company barbecue that night, and that he wanted all employees to make an effort to be there.

Arriving at Herndon Park, where the barbecue was being held, Lila spotted a group of females and knew Ted Carmike would be in the center of them. Smiling to herself, she headed for the tables to put down the dinner rolls she'd been asked to pick up on her way. Instead of joining the crowd around Ted Carmike, she headed for her favorite spot, a little gazebo beside a stream that flowed through the park. She sat down on a bench and took a deep breath, then slowly let it out. She could feel tension drain from her as she listened to the little natural waterfall close to the gazebo. She closed her eyes and felt herself starting to relax. Tomorrow was Saturday. No work. No plans. What a wonderful feeling!

She smelled the cologne before she heard his footstep on the wooden gazebo. She opened her eyes just in time to watch Ted Carmike sit on the seat opposite her.

"Hi," he said, smiling impishly.

"Where are all your admirers?" she asked, wondering what he was doing here, interrupting her moment.

"I sneaked away when I saw you headed down here. I told them I had to go to the little boy's room."

"Why?" She wasn't being obnoxious. She was really curious why he would come to her when so many beautiful women were falling at his feet.

"Are you married?" He ignored her question.

"No," she answered. Then remembered, "And I'm not the one who asked you that question this morning."

"I know. But I wanted you to know I wasn't married."

"Why?" she asked again, really feeling baffled.

But again ignoring her question, he asked, "Do you have a name?" His apparent amusement made his eyes crinkle around the corners.

"Lila Chestnut," she answered. Glancing around, she realized the sun had gone down and the automatic lights had come on around the picnic area. The lighting threw the gazebo into shadow and she knew the people who were starting to gather around the tables to get their food could barely see her and Ted.

"How appropriate," Ted's voice interrupted her thoughts. At her questioning glance, he continued, "Your name and your hair color are the same."

"Oh that," she chuckled, self-consciously pushing a strand of hair back into place. "You know," she added, "they're going to be wondering where you are. They're beginning to eat. You'd better go up there and mingle."

"What about you? Aren't you going to eat?" As she shook her head in the negative, he continued, "Then I'm not, either. I'm not going up there unless you do."

"Why? Why aren't you up there soaking up all the interest you've generated just by being here?"

"Hasn't it occurred to you yet that I want to be with you?"

Lila was surprised at the gentleness in his voice, and her eyes flew to meet his. She felt her pulses unexpectedly quicken. She was struggling to find words to answer when Charlotte's voice shouted close to them, "Here they are, down here in the dark! Lila, shame on you for trying to keep Ted all to yourself! You two come on up here."

"We'll continue this later," he promised, and held his hand out to support her as she stepped out of the gazebo.

As they climbed the slight incline back to the group of people waiting for them, she was intensely aware of Ted's hand in the center of her back, gently guiding her.

As soon as they reached the group, he was once again surrounded by adoring females. Lila slipped away unnoticed and went home.

The weekend she had looked forward to was spent obsessing over Ted Carmike's words under the gazebo. It just didn't make sense. Why would a man as handsome as he was single her out when he could have anyone he wanted? Sure, she'd had relationships, and she'd dated handsome men, but most of them couldn't get past the fact that she was somewhat larger than this society's "perfect woman" type, the slim female form they were used to seeing plastered everywhere they looked. So why would a handsome, successful business tycoon like Ted Carmike want to spend time with her? Was he just trying to find out something about her that would justify his action if he decided to let her go from her position?

The more she tried to forget the incident, the more her mind returned to it. By Monday she was dreading going back to the office and facing him.

At ten o'clock sharp Monday morning, Lila was called to Mr. Hoffman's office. She was disappointed to see Ted Carmike sitting in one of the chairs in the office.

"Have a seat, Lila. Ted and I want to talk with you." She was immediately aware of the sinking sensation in the pit of her stomach. *This is it,* she thought.

"First, I want to assure you, even though I think you know it, that I consider you to be an exceptional employee. You have never given me cause to regret hiring you, and you have been the best secretary that I've ever had, personally."

"But?" Lila knew what was coming. She tried to ignore the sweat forming in her palms. How could this be happening to her?

"But," here Ted took over. "We're going to have to transfer you to another office."

"Another office? We don't have another office!" She could feel her anger rising now. She just wanted to have this humiliating meeting over with so she could get out of here before she embarrassed herself by losing her temper and saying something she would regret.

"Yes, we do have other offices. We've just this week acquired the Dillingham offices over on Seventh Avenue. Are you familiar with that area?"

"Sure," she answered. Everyone was familiar with the swankiest law offices in the city.

"Well, we need someone there who knows how we want things done at the Fessler's Group offices, so we're sending you over there."

"But why me? I'm not the only one who knows how things are done at Fessler's Group. In fact, I'm not even the best person for the job," she argued.

"But you're the one we've chosen." Ted's voice was all business, and Lila sensed if she wanted to keep her job, she'd best cooperate. She felt a small sense of relief that she was just being transferred, not terminated.

"So when do I go over there?" Resignation filled her voice, causing the two men to glance at each other.

"Tomorrow," Ted answered. "We'll move everything from your office here that you'll need. You won't have to worry with anything. Just be there at nine o'clock in the morning. I'll be there to introduce you and help you get adjusted."

"Gee, that's kind of you." She couldn't keep the touch of sarcasm from her voice as she left the room.

"Are you sure this is going to be okay?" Mr. Hoffman asked Ted, as Lila dejectedly left the room.

"It has to be this way, Jack. You know company policy, and you know how I feel about her."

"I hope you know what you're doing," the older man said.

Lila slammed the door to her apartment as she entered.

"It's my weight!" she yelled at the walls. "That's the only thing it could be! My work is good. My work record is good. Mr. Hoffman said he was pleased. That Ted Carmike just wants me out of the office because I'm the only one that doesn't fit the stereotype. That has to be the reason!"

Well, in the morning when she saw him, she would just come right out and ask him. She'd heard of this type of discrimination, but she'd never been the brunt of it. She'd always dressed carefully, tried to look her best, and she'd never been turned down for a job because of her size before. She sure as hell wasn't going to lose the position she had just because some good-looking, smug Don Juan came swooping into her office and thought he could beautify the place by getting rid of her!

The next morning, Lila spent more time than usual getting dressed. She put on her best business dress, and her hair and makeup were impeccable. Anger added a glaze to her green eyes, and she'd received several admiring glances by the time she reached the Dillingham office building.

As she stepped off the elevator, she saw Ted standing at the receptionist's desk. The receptionist, blond and svelte, was looking up at him with her heart in her eyes.

At the sound of the elevator doors swooshing open, Ted turned and looked at Lila.

"There you are! I was waiting on you. Wow! You look gorgeous this morning!"

"Save it!" snapped Lila. "Where's my new office?"

"Now, there's an entrance, if I've ever seen one," remarked Ted, leading Lila to an impressive large office that was beautifully decorated.

Closing the door none too quietly, Lila turned on him.

"Now I want to know the real reason that I have to leave Fessler's Group. I want to hear it from your own lips, if you've got the guts to say it!"

"Okay. I'm sure you're aware of the company policy on dating co-workers. I can't date you as long as you work in the same office with me. And I knew as soon as I saw you step into the elevator Friday morning that I wanted to date you. So, will you have dinner with me tonight?" The warmth in his voice flowed through Lila like a soothing balm.

"Oh," she whispered, sinking into the nearest chair.

Freedom

Molly's green eyes devoured the handsome face before her. Mike was everything she'd ever dreamed of in a man. He had the body of a Greek god, and a face that could stop the heart of any woman. She loved being seen with him. She knew she became the envy of any woman who looked her way when she was with Mike. He made her complete.

"Well, what's your answer?" Mike's voice interrupted Molly's thoughts.

Looking down in disbelief at the huge diamond he'd slipped onto her finger, she answered, "Yes, Mike, I'll marry you."

He smiled that boyish smile she loved, and then asked the question she'd been dreading.

"Just when are you going to take me to meet your family? We've been dating for six months and you've never taken me to eat one of your mother's wonderful meals that you rave about."

Molly had not been quite honest with Mike about her family background. Her mother was a plus-size woman. Her sister was a plus-size woman. And Molly had to starve herself constantly, or she, too, would be plus-sized.

Suddenly she wished she had found out earlier in their relationship how Mike felt about this subject, but for some reason, she'd been afraid of the answer.

"We could probably spend the day with them on Sunday," she replied, trying to keep the doubt from her voice. "That's when Mom does her best cooking. I'll call and let her know we're coming. They've been after me to let them meet you."

Mike's loving gaze made Molly wonder how she could ever have doubted his love for her.

The diamond glistened and caught both their attention. A low chuckle rumbled from Mike as he entwined his fingers into her hair and brought her face to his for a kiss. Then, together, they walked out into the cold December night.

Sunday morning came too soon for Molly. Her family was thrilled she was engaged, and her mother had invited the entire family to have Sunday dinner with them and meet Molly's new fiancé. She had even invited Aunt Maggie, who was a super plus-size woman.

To Molly's horror, for the first time in her life she felt ashamed of her beloved family.

Every one welcomed Mike with open arms, and he seemed to relax and enjoy himself. Molly couldn't help but notice that he spent a lot of time talking with her sister, Nell.

Nell was a successful model for the plus-size fashion industry, and she also gave motivational lectures for women of size. Many times she had encouraged Molly to let go of self-destructive dieting habits and to just eat healthily and be content with the weight she wound up being. But Molly would only laugh at Nell, two years her senior, and kid her about trying to boss her around.

After good-byes were said and Mike was driving Molly home, he was unusually quiet.

Finally, Molly asked, "Did you enjoy the day?"

As an answer, Mike asked without looking at her, "Molly, are you the only woman in your family that isn't fat?"

Molly felt a pending doom.

"I've never really thought about it," she lied in a quiet voice, "but I may very well be."

Nothing else was said until Mike stopped the car in her driveway. Then, turning to her, he said, "Molly, promise me you won't get fat after we're married."

"Mike! I can't promise you such a thing! People gain weight because of a lot of reasons. Women gain weight after having babies, sometimes. Or—or—sometimes people gain weight for seemingly no reason at all." She could feel desperation growing inside her.

"NO! I won't be married to a fat woman! You should have been up front with me on our first date," he ground out.

"And how would that have played out, Mike? How should I have handled that? Should I have said, 'Hi, my name is Molly, I'm not fat now, but I come from a long line of fat females, so if you don't like fat women, maybe this should be our last date.' Or maybe I should wear a locket around my neck with a picture of all my fat relatives in it? How should I have handled it, Mike?"

"Just get out of the car, Molly. I have to do some serious thinking about us."

Freedom

Too stunned to reply, Molly jumped out of the car and ran to her door. Mike drove away before she even got the door unlocked.

She slumped across her bed. She couldn't believe her engagement of four days had already ended like this. Quietly, the tears started. She had no idea how long she cried before she slept.

The next morning, she called a courier and sent her engagement ring back to Mike with a brief note that simply said, "Have a good life."

Then she called her sister. "Nell, I'm ready to find out who I really am, but I'm going to need a lot of help.

The two sisters smiled at each other as the waiter set down a slice of cheesecake for each of them.

"So what are we celebrating?" Nell asked.

Molly lingered a moment as the first bite of cheesecake melted in her mouth. "One year ago today, at this very table, Mike proposed to me."

"So *that's* what this is all about! I know you don't usually indulge in cheesecake unless there's a really good reason."

They laughed together, as they had done many times in the past year.

"You've come a long way, baby," Nell said, looking lovingly at her sister. "Look at you now. You're beautiful! But it took us quite some time to convince you of that, huh?"

Molly looked affectionately back at her sister. Her friend. Her inspiration. Nell had helped her learn good, healthy eating habits. She had insisted Molly join the exercise program she taught at the local YMCA. But in spite of all her healthy lifestyle changes, Molly slowly started to gain weight. Because for Molly, the only way she could keep from gaining weight was to stay hungry every hour of every day.

She had decided a year ago that she didn't want to spend her life hungry. Life was too short to be miserable all the time.

Nell had continually reassured her that she was beautiful, but most important of all, she was healthy. Nell also assured her that she'd reach a stopping point and not gain any more weight once she reached her natural set-point weight. The weight she was genetically programmed to be.

Molly had enrolled in a clothes-designing class and now had a growing business, designing plus-size fashions for a local dressmaker. She hoped to start her own line soon.

Yes, she'd come a long way, but what she felt the best about was that she was at total peace with both her inner-self and her outer-self. She finally knew who she was.

"Molly?" She'd been so involved with her thoughts she hadn't noticed the man walk up.

"Mike!"

"May I sit down?" he asked, shyly.

"Sure," she said, skeptically.

"You're beautiful," he said quietly. He, too, had changed. His face was gaunt and his eyes had shadows under them. Molly realized now that the face she had once thought so handsome was actually a weak face, with spoiled and petty features.

"Molly, please forgive me. I can't get you out of my mind. I don't care if you're fat! I love you. I need you in my life."

Slowly, Molly stood and looked down at the man she once thought she loved.

"Mike, you're a year too late. I'm sorry." And she walked out into the cold December night.

Nell spoke behind her. "Are you okay?"

"Dear Nell, I've never been better! But if you don't mind, I'd like to be alone." Molly started walking the few blocks to her duplex. The wind lifted and tousled her hair. She turned her face into the cold, cleansing breeze, and was filled with joy. She was free! After a year of doubt and wondering, she knew she didn't need Mike to make her feel worthwhile. She didn't have to rely on someone else to give her the self-esteem she needed.

And the next person she gave her heart to would love her *because*, not *in spite* of, who and what she was.

The Clock

From her vantage point as she sat perched on the stool behind the counter, Veronica's blue-gray eyes slowly perused the shelves and racks of old treasures in the small antique shop where she worked.

As her eyes made their way around the walls, they stopped at an old clock that was shoved into the corner of a back shelf. It was brass, with bells on top that sounded an alarm. It reminded her of the wind-up clock that had always been in her grandmother's home when she was a child. The soft ticking of that old clock had lulled her to sleep many nights.

Wondering if this one would sound the same, or if it still even worked, she slid off the stool and retrieved the clock from its resting place. She sat back down and slowly twisted the dull key on the back. She was happy to hear a strong "tick-tock, tick-tock" begin.

Feeling as if she had discovered an old friend, she decided to see if the alarm still worked. Glancing at her watch, she set the time,

11:45, then set the alarm for noon and pulled the stem out.

Just then the door opened and two elderly ladies walked in. They shopped for a little while, bought a few items, then left.

Veronica was closing the drawer to the cash register when the alarm went off. She had momentarily forgotten the clock, and the sharp clanging of the alarm startled her. She was surprised and happy that even the alarm still worked. But almost instantly she realized something was wrong with the sound of the alarm. Instead of making a *"ding, ding, ding, ding"* sound when the clapper hit the bell on each side, the sound was *"ding, chunk, ding, chunk."* Something was muting the tone of the right bell.

She pushed the stem in to shut the alarm off. Turning the clock upside down, she tried to see what was causing the problem. She could barely see what looked like a piece of paper inside the dome of the bell. Cautiously, she ran a fingernail around the inside of the bell, and felt the paper move a little. Very gently, being careful not to tear or damage it, she slowly worked the piece of folded paper out.

Excitement started to build inside her as she looked at the age-yellowed folded paper in her hand. Slowly and gently, feeling as if she were invading someone's privacy, she unfolded the paper to reveal dim writing that had faded with time.

Going to the window for more light, she held the note at an angle and read:

> *We will find our treasure in the old house on Maple Street. Meet me at six o'clock. V.*

Surely the "old house on Maple Street" couldn't be the old Mabry mansion! That old house had been grown up with weeds since

Veronica could remember. But—maybe this note was written *before* she could remember!

Excitement gripped her. How could she find out the age of this paper? Was the "treasure" still in the old house? Did she dare go look for it?

She remembered that Mrs. Frampton, the owner of the shop, always labeled her items as to when, where, and from whom she had purchased each piece. Veronica practically ran to the file cabinet and looked under "c" for clock. To her satisfaction, after scanning several descriptions she found the information about the clock—a neatly printed name and address. *John Meadows' estate sale—304 Tulip Lane.* But that still didn't tell her how old the note was.

She couldn't leave the shop today, but she only worked until noon tomorrow. She would go to the address on Tulip Lane. She didn't have a plan, but she felt compelled to look the address up and talk with someone.

At 12 o'clock sharp the next day Veronica was on her way to delve into the mystery that had haunted her all night.

Since Tulip Lane wasn't far from the antique shop, she decided to walk. It was a beautiful spring day, and she pushed back a tendril of hair the gentle breeze caused to playfully caress her cheek. Today she wore her auburn, naturally curly hair arranged on top of her head. It was her grandmother's favorite style, because it reminded her grandmother of her youngest sister. Grandmere always said Veronica was the mirror image of her baby sister, Veronica's great aunt. She'd inherited her aunt's full, voluptuous figure. And she'd even been named after her great aunt, whose life had ended tragically when, as a young woman, she had saved a child's life, losing her own in the process.

Veronica turned down Tulip Lane and soon found #304. The house stood large and beautiful and spoke of quiet, unflaunted wealth. As she approached, she realized that a wreath of fresh flowers hung on the front door.

Veronica's excitement at finding the house subsided when she saw the wreath. There had been a death in the family. Should she intrude or just go away? No. She had come this far. She just had to find out something about that note.

As she was about the ring the doorbell, she noticed a card on the flowers. It read:

"Macon's Funeral Home—407 Tulip Lane."

Feeling that she was intruding but not able to stop herself, Veronica proceeded down the street until she found the funeral home. As she entered, an attendant approached her. "I'm looking for the Meadows family," Veronica said in a hushed voice.

"They left about five minutes ago," he told her apologetically. "They're going to Mallory Memorial Cemetery."

Veronica was very familiar with the cemetery. Her great aunt Veronica was buried there. Her grandmother would be buried there, and she was sure she would be buried there also.

"May I call a cab?" she asked the attendant, who pointed to a phone.

In less than 20 minutes Veronica was at the gate of the cemetery. Following her instructions, the cab driver drove slowly into the memorial park. The headstones were a mixture of grand old monuments crumbling with the wearing of time, and the gleaming new granite stones of those who had recently joined their ancestors.

This day there was only one group in the entire cemetery, so Veronica instructed the driver to let her out a little distance from the graveside gathering.

She made her way slowly through the graves, being very careful not to draw attention to herself. When she came within the sound of the minister's voice, she stopped. She vaguely heard the minister mention John Meadows' name, so she knew she was in the right place.

She stopped beside an old monument of an angel that was taller than she was. The gray color of her crepe-de-chine dress blended with the gray monument so well that she almost seemed part of the gravestone itself.

From her inconspicuous position, she watched the procedures. She decided that the man at the end of the front row must be somehow in charge of the gathering. She studied the man as he listened to the service. His hair was dark, with just enough gray at the temples to make him distinguished looking. She guessed him to be in his early thirties. Probably the grandson of John Meadows. Hopefully, he would know something about the note.

As the service drew to a close, Veronica wondered how she would approach the man. She supposed she would just walk up to him and tell him the story of the clock and note, and hope he would talk to her about it. She knew she was crossing all boundaries of courtesy for the situation, but for some reason she felt driven, unable to stop herself.

Just as the minister said, "let us pray," the man she planned to talk to turned and looked directly into her eyes. She saw his body jolt, and sensed his sharply in-drawn breath. She believed she could see the color drain from his face even at this distance!

Their eyes locked. Surely she imagined the recognition, disbelief, and confusion playing on his face.

As the crowd began to disperse, the man walked slowly toward her. Veronica wanted to move to meet him, but she felt pinned to her spot by the piercing gaze of his dark brown eyes. He stopped within a few feet of her, and asked, "Veronica?" Disbelief was in full evidence in his deep voice.

"Yes, but how do you know my name?" Veronica's naturally husky voice was even more hushed now, because of the situation.

The man took a step closer and reached out tentatively and touched her face.

"But you're real!" he said, as if she might argue with him.

Her chuckle was genuine. "Yes, I do believe so."

"But how?" As he spoke, he stared at the monument above her head.

Slowly, Veronica turned and read the inscription on the monument:

Veronica Macey
Born 1906
Died 1926
She gave us 20 beautiful years.

Veronica, without realizing it, had waited beside her great aunt's grave. She hadn't been here since she was a child, when she would come with her grandmother, so she hadn't even realized where she had stopped.

The man was still staring at her. It dawned on her that he believed she was the Veronica who was buried beneath their feet. But how could he possibly know her Aunt Veronica? He was much, much too young to have known her in person.

"My name is Veronica Macey Harting. She was my great aunt, my namesake, and I'm told I look just like she did. And now it's your turn. How on earth would you know anything about her?"

A look of pure relief swept over the man's face. He indicated a bench close by. "Could we sit down, please? My knees are sort of weak." He smiled for the first time, and Veronica was impressed by the strength he seemed to possess even as he admitted to a weakness.

As they sat down, he explained. "My name is John Meadows III. That's my grandfather that we just buried." He looked at the grave now being filled with fresh dirt. His face was sad and thoughtful as he watched the last shovel of earth land on the mound. Then he turned back to Veronica.

"But why are you here? If you didn't know you were beside your aunt's grave, apparently you weren't visiting her."

Suddenly, Veronica remembered the note and why she was here. She explained to him about the clock, the note, and how her search had led her here.

Again his face held disbelief. "So that's where Grandpa's clock ended up! You see, Grandma died about five and a half years ago, and Grandpa let her sisters clear her things away. Well, they had an estate sale and went a little overboard. They sold some of Grandpa's things, and one of them was the clock. That clock was a precious thing to him, and he never got over losing it."

At Veronica's questioning look, he continued. "When I was around eight years old, I loved pretending I was a spy. I sneaked around and spied on everyone. One day Grandma left the house and I was spying on Grandpa. He went over to the mantle, took the clock down, took a note out of it and read it. Then he just sat and stared into space with the saddest look on his face I had ever seen. He sat for a long time, then he put the note back in the bell of the clock and put the clock back on the shelf. From then on, every time I got a chance, when Grandpa was alone I would watch him follow the same procedure.

"Then one day I followed him here. He knelt here, beside Veronica's grave, and placed a bouquet of roses on it. Then he sat here, on this bench, for a long time with that same sad look on his face. He would never have discovered me, but I had unknowingly knelt in an ant bed to spy on him. When the ants started stinging me, I started dancing and yelling. He rescued me, and then because he felt he owed me an explanation, he told me his story. It became "our secret." And he showed me a faded photograph he kept hidden in a secret compartment of his wallet. That photo looked just like you. Or should I say, you look just like it."

"But I don't understand," Veronica said, urging him to go on with his story.

"Grandpa and your Aunt Veronica were very young and very much in love. So much in love that they just could not stay apart. The only problem was that their fathers hated each other, and forbade the young lovers to date. But your aunt and my grandfather decided to take matters into their own hands. My grandfather secretly bought the old house on Maple Street and together they quietly fixed it up inside, but left it looking old and unkempt on the outside, so no one would become suspicious. The note you found was from your great aunt to my grandfather. 'The treasure' that she referred to was their wedding. She had arranged for a minister to meet them there that night and marry them. But as I'm sure you know, on her way to meet

Grandpa and the minister, she saw a small child standing in the path of a runaway horse. She ran to save the child, and did, but the horse trampled her. Ever since then, once a year, on this very date of his burial, Grandpa would bring flowers and sit with his beloved Veronica for a while. And now, he will always be here close to her."

The man stood. Taking the red rose from his lapel, he went and placed it on the first Veronica's grave. "From Grandpa," he said quietly to the angelic monument.

Then, looking at Veronica, he asked, "Do you want to go somewhere for dinner? We have a lot to talk about."

She put her hand in his outstretched one. As they walked away, both knew that some unseen force had determined that John Meadows' and Veronica Macey's love would yet live.

 Playboy

Ava sat at her desk quietly sipping a cup of hot coffee. An amused smile was on her full lips as she watched the office hubbub.

There was a new excitement at Brown & Brown this morning. An almost tangible current exuded from the chattering secretaries. Everyone had on her best office apparel, makeup was faultless, and there was not a hair out of place on any head.

A new office manager was arriving this morning, but not just any new office manager. The son of the first Mr. Brown of "Brown & Brown had been transferred here to the main office.

Excited rumor had it that this Rod Brown was extremely handsome, loads of fun, and, of course, filthy rich.

Ava's smile deepened, slowly. How many times in her six years of secretarial work had she seen this scene repeated? And usually the outcome was the same.

Playboy

The young playboy would come in, sweep each girl off her feet, either in unison or one at a time, then he would either be gone or married to a girl from "back home."

Ava was not a skeptic, but she was practical. And she had two things going for her. She did not like playboys, and, as a rule, playboys didn't like her.

Her full, voluptuous figure gave testimony to the fact that Ava didn't care for crash diets or the fashion designers who dictated that she had to look like Olive Oyle in order to be accepted in their society. What Ava did care for was a well-balanced diet, good exercise, and beautifully designed clothes that stated to the world she had good taste and that she was at home and happy in her body.

She knew that to some of her co-workers she was considered, as she had overheard one whisper behind her hand, "fat." But that didn't bother her, either. The word fat, after all, was just an adjective. Just like short, tall, or slim.

So the playboys who came and went limited their attention to staring at and probably fantasizing about Ava, but it just wasn't cool to be seen with a larger woman. Why, what would their friends think?

"And what are you smiling about?"

Startled, Ava looked up at the small redhead standing beside her desk. Nettie was naturally petite, and the nicest girl in the office.

"Oh, I was just watching everyone get ready for the big entrance the new boy will make," Ava answered.

"Boy?" Nettie asked. "I don't exactly call thirty-five a boy."

"Well I didn't know he was thirty-five, but you know how those guys are. They never grow up. He probably acts just like a spoiled brat."

"Oh, you're just being a sour-puss," Nettie came back with fake consternation. "Come on, loosen up. Here, I'll help you. Listen to this new joke I heard last night."

The women were so involved in the joke that they didn't realize the subject of all the excitement had finally arrived. The joke turned out to have one of those really clever punch lines, and Ava, having a good sense of humor, was caught off guard by the story. Suddenly her laughter pealed out in the quiet office, startling everyone, including herself—for at that moment she looked across the room into the eyes of one of the most fascinating men she had ever seen.

The eyes that seemed to hold hers against her will were such a light green they almost looked like translucent glass. He was a little above average height. His coal black, slightly wavy hair was beginning to gray at the temples.

As Ava's brown eyes finished roaming the body across the room and came back to the translucent green ones, the newcomer slightly bowed to her before turning to his father, who was introducing him to everyone.

Had he actually winked or had Ava just imagined it?

After being properly introduced, Rod Brown disappeared into his father's office to be briefed on everything in general, and didn't reappear for the rest of the day.

Ava continued with her first plan for the day, which was to finish her work as quickly as possible so she could leave early and do some shopping. Nettie was having a party tonight and had asked Ava if she'd help her play hostess to all the guests. But as luck would have it, a long string of little time-consuming, irritating incidents occurred throughout the day, causing Ava to find herself sitting in the big room of computers and desks alone, long after all the other secretaries had left for the day.

She was addressing her last envelope when, gradually, she became aware she was being watched. She finished the envelope, tucked the letter inside, sealed it, and laid it on the desk before she looked up.

There, not ten feet from her, stood Rod Brown, leaning against a desk with his arms crossed across his chest and an amused look in those devastating eyes.

"Well, are you overly diligent, or just slow?" he asked without moving from his position.

"Just slow," answered Ava, as she casually turned off her computer and started to gather her personal stuff to take home with her. It was obvious that she didn't intend to be intimidated.

"That's not what I hear from your superiors," came the cool, relaxed voice. She liked the deep, resonant sound of it.

"Oh?" Ava's eyes flashed to meet his as fast as her question.

"You're surprised? Oh, I don't really believe that. I'm told you're quite efficient in here, and I sort of think you already know that."

Ava was becoming a little embarrassed. She wanted this conversation to be over.

"Yes," she answered matter of factly. "I know I'm good. Do you want to know why?"

For an answer he just looked at her with an amused twinkle in those magnetic green eyes.

And because Ava felt she was on shaky ground, almost as if he were deliberately trying to intimidate her, she felt her anger starting to rise. She suddenly had a desire to have this conversation over, and to get away from this person.

"I'm good, Playboy, because I make it a point to be good. Is there any other way?"

"Are you ready to go, Rod?" His father's voice interrupted any comment he might have had. So instead of answering her, his eyes leisurely perused her entire length, before he turned to join his father.

Ava sighed blissfully as she lay back in the hot tub of water. Just a few quiet moments to relax before time to dress for the party was all she asked.

The party—the usual, boring party.

Ava knew one day she would find a good man, but sometimes she so longed for that time in her life to arrive. She relaxed lazily as hot water gently swirled and covered her nude body.

It seemed only a moment or two later that she was brought hastily back to consciousness by the sharp ringing of the phone. As she sat up in the tub, she noticed that the water was cool. *Oh, no!* She'd fallen asleep. She grabbed a towel and headed for the phone.

"Hello?"

"Ava! Why are you still at home?" Nettie's slightly irritated voice came from the other end of the line.

"I fell asleep in the tub," Ava answered guiltily.

"You *whaaaat?* How could you? The guests are already arriving!"

"Okay, okay! I'll be there in twenty minutes." As Ava hung up the phone, she removed her towel. *What a mess,* she thought as she rushed toward the closet. No time to set her hair. Ha! No time to even blow-dry her hair.

Standing before the mirror, she shrugged her shoulders and started arranging her chocolate brown hair in a twist on top of her head, taking care to leave a few curly tendrils loose around her face and the back of her neck. Then after quickly applying her makeup, she slipped into the first thing her hands fell on when she reached into the "dressy" end of her closet. A straight red dress with a white jacket.

Ava always felt confident in this outfit. The lacy collar of the dress rose high around her neck, and went perfectly with the way she'd fixed her hair.

In just nineteen minutes she was dashing up the steps to Nettie's front door. As she reached for the doorknob, the door was pulled open and again Ava found herself staring into the eyes of Rod Brown. Why did Nettie have to invite him?

The magnetic force that seemed to lock her eyes to his and pull her toward him was so strong that it made her throat ache.

"Well, finally!" came Nettie's indignant voice from behind Rod. "Did Sleeping Beauty finally get here?"

Nettie's interruption broke the locked eyes and both people turned to her. Rod was the first to speak. "I'd better run my errand and let you women work this out." He ran toward a small red sports car parked by the curb.

"I'm so sorry." Ava sounded so earnest that Nettie broke into a big smile.

"Oh, forget it, honey, everything's fine. In fact, I really don't even need you."

"Now you tell me, after I've almost killed myself getting here," Ava playfully admonished her friend.

Both women made their way into the kitchen. Ava spoke to people she passed, and was amused at how "dolled up" the women from the office were. As she and Nettie stepped into the kitchen, Ava commented, "Boy, everybody sure has their best face on, don't they?"

"Yeah, including yourself."

Ava's laugh was genuine. "Are you kidding? My hair is still wet, my makeup barely got on, and I put on the first thing my hands touched in the closet."

"Well, Rod seemed to like what he saw," was Nettie's reply.

"Nettie, you're always looking for something, aren't you? You beat all I've ever seen!"

"We'll see," Nettie answered smugly as she left the kitchen.

Ava set about to finish making the hors d'oeuvres someone had started. When that task was finished, she loaded a few dishes into the dishwasher, then started to make the avocado dip Nettie wanted.

After searching through the refrigerator twice, she closed the door with an exasperated slam and said aloud, "Well, how am I supposed to make avocado dip without avocados?"

"Is this what you're looking for?" came a deep voice close behind her.

Ava was so startled that she jumped visibly. Instantly, she recognized the voice, and just as instantly she was angry. Turning to face the cause of her discomfort, she said irritably, "Is this sneaking up on people something you've learned from spying on your employees, or do you just do it for fun?" She expected anything but the loud laugh that escaped from the man standing in front of her.

"Well put, and much deserved," Rod answered, placing the avocados on the counter. "Really, I'm sorry. I didn't mean to startle you. Why don't I help you make the dip?"

"No, you have a room full of pretty young things out there just waiting for you to come and amuse yourself with them. Go, before they storm the kitchen."

"I'd rather help you make dip." His voice was teasing.

"Sure, Playboy, sure," Ava said in a patronizing voice as she turned and reached for one of the avocados on the counter. As her hand covered the avocado, Rod's hand covered hers. Her first thought was how masculine his hand looked and how perfectly it covered hers, and that his other hand was on her waist. His breath was a gentle caress as he spoke softly into her ear. She felt her pulses leap. What was wrong with her? She didn't usually react like a school-girl to this type of come-on.

"When's the dip gonna be ready?" A shout from the door brought them back to reality.

"Damn!" Rod said under his breath, then aloud, "Nettie, you do have bad timing, y'know that?"

"Oh, hello, Rod!" chirped Nettie, as if he hadn't even spoken. "Celia said for you to come there. She wants to tell you something."

As Rod reluctantly left the room, Nettie turned to Ava with a knowing look on her face.

"Come on and make the dip and keep your mouth closed!" warned Ava, before Nettie could utter what she was thinking.

"Yeah, we've got to get you out there in the crowd," Nettie answered with the same look.

Soon the dip was finished and Ava and Nettie were trying to make their way through the dancers and merrymakers with their trays of "goodies." They were about to set the trays of food down on the serving table when Ava heard a familiar voice close beside her.

"Here, let me help you." And the tray was placed on the table for her.

"Like to dance?" Before she could answer she was gathered close in Rod Brown's arms and guided into a swaying motion.

"What if I had said no?" she asked, feeling almost too bashful to look at the man at such a close range.

"I would have ignored you," he smiled down at her.

Ava was aware her heart was pounding. She hoped desperately that he couldn't feel it. As she glanced over his shoulder in hopes of gaining her composure, she became acutely aware of jealous female eyes watching her. So she just closed her eyes and concentrated on the beautiful music drifting through the air.

When the music stopped and Ava opened her eyes, she realized they were beside the glass doors that led to the balcony. Rod held her hand and led her outside. A soft spring breeze brought the promise of summer as it ruffled the loose curls around her face.

"The moon's full tonight," Rod said, as he gazed at the sky.

"How do you tell the moon from the street lights? I haven't really seen the moon since I came to this big city." There was a wistful note in Ava's voice as she gently removed her hand from his.

"I know where there's a place outside of town where the moon shines brighter than anywhere in the world. Let's drive out there and I'll prove it to you." He took her hand and started for the door.

But Ava pulled back and asked suspiciously, "How can you know of a place outside of town when you only got here today?"

"I grew up here," he answered.

"You what?"

"I grew up here. My father owns a thousand-acre ranch ten miles out of town. I'm actually a country boy." The breeze tousling his hair made his statement almost believable, but suddenly Ava remembered who he really was. She also realized with total clarity that she was rapidly headed for quicksand.

"Sure, Playboy, you're as much a country boy as I am a poor little rich girl. We'd better go inside." She started to pass him to go back to the party, but he caught her arm and turned her to face him. "Okay, what is this 'playboy' stuff? That makes several times that you've called me that today."

"That's what you are, isn't it? You're rich, single, handsome, and you drive a little red convertible sports car. That adds up to a playboy in my book."

"Do you always judge people instantly like this? You don't seem like that kind of person to me." The puzzled look on Rod's face was genuine.

"Well, you know what they say about first impressions," was Ava's lame answer.

"I can't help it if my father happened to be a successful man, but I'm proud that I'm able to follow in his footsteps. And, yes, I'm single—because my wife ran off with another man eight years ago. As far as being handsome, I understand that a person can be a so-called 'playboy' no matter how they look, and dammit, I just happen to like little red convertibles."

"Okay, okay, so maybe I was wrong. I'm sorry. But why are you wasting time on me when there's a room full of women in there falling all over themselves to impress you? You should have seen the jealous looks I was getting when we were dancing."

"Wasting time? Why do you call it wasting time just because I want to be with you? Ava," he said, stepping closer to her and gently touching her cheek with the back of his fingers. She could feel the sprinkling of hair on his fingers gently brush her face. "I'm attracted to you. Does that bother you?"

"It doesn't bother me," she answered, feeling the warmth flow through her at his admission that he was attracted to her. "It just doesn't fit the pattern."

"Doesn't fit what pattern? Look, you've got me all wrong on this playboy stuff. I'm really not just looking for a one-night stand."

"That's not the pattern I'm talking about. Men like you don't usually go for women like me."

"What are you talking about?"

"I'm talking about my size, Rod. I'm not the typical slim model type that guys like you want to have clinging to their arms."

"No, you're not the typical slim model type. You're one hell of a woman! Curves everywhere the eye can see! You make my blood run hot just looking at you. To each his own, Ava, but personally, I like a voluptuous, curvaceous woman, just like I like red sports cars."

Rod put both hands on Ava's shoulders and pulled her closer. He gazed down into her eyes and said softly, "Look at you. You're beautiful. You look soft and warm and alluring, and you felt so good when I held you in my arms. Give me a chance, Ava. Let me prove that I'm not your typical playboy."

As he gently kissed her, Ava knew they would go for that country drive and the moon would be bright there tonight. Maybe brighter than it had ever been for her.

The Promise of Winter

Julia was bombarded with mixed emotions as she watched several of her friends climb onto the backs of the horses of their choice. They turned and waved to her as they proceeded to follow the guide down the trail. Initially, she'd thought that visiting Dawson's Dude Ranch and Resort was a good idea when her friends had suggested it. But she hadn't counted on her attack of last-minute nerves.

"Why didn't you go with them?"

Julia turned, startled by the voice, to look at the man who had come up behind her. He was of average height, with wavy black hair and friendly gray eyes. He was wearing jeans, a cowboy shirt, and cowboy boots, and was slowly twirling a Stetson in his hands.

As Julia finished the tour of his body and came back to his now-smiling eyes, he winked slowly and repeated his question.

"Why aren't you with your friends?"

"I—I don't like horses," she replied, wondering why she suddenly felt uncomfortable.

"Why?"

"Well—I really do like horses—I'm just not in the mood to ride today."

"Why?" Now the amusement in his eyes had spread to the beginning of a grin on his sensuous mouth.

Julia realized the stranger was deliberately taunting her, and she was suddenly annoyed.

"Actually, it's none of your business why I'm not with my friends or whether I like horses or not! And I don't have to answer your questions! So go away and do stop looking at me like that!"

Now there was a full grin on the handsome face, causing the man to look mischievous and reckless. "I'm sorry," he apologized, extending his hand. "I'm Mike Dawson. I'm one of the guides here." He held her hand as he continued to talk. "I don't usually harass our visitors, but I overheard your friends trying to coax you on a horse and I overheard your reason for not wanting to go."

Julia slowly pulled her hand from his as she felt her face becoming hot, now from embarrassment instead of the anger she'd felt earlier.

She hadn't wanted to go on the trail ride because of her weight, and she had very eloquently told her friends that if she tried to get on a horse, the horse and saddle both would probably wind up on top of her!

"Wait—please. I didn't come over here to embarrass you." His voice was soft now, and he had stepped closer. Julia felt slightly flustered to feel the sudden quickening of her pulses.

He reached out and touched her shoulder. "Come on and see the horses. If you decide to ride one, we have mounting steps for people who don't like to swing up with the stirrups. Come on and pet the horses."

Julia could hear the earnestness in his voice, so she smiled for the first time since they'd met and said, with a shrug of her shoulders, "Why not?"

She stood up from the wooden bench she'd been sitting on and started to walk in the direction Mike indicated.

She, too, wore jeans and boots, and a western-style pullover top tucked into her jeans. Her clothes fit her ample curves beautifully, but she wasn't aware of Mike's appreciative smile as he followed her into the stables.

Julia could do anything with her extra pounds that most women could do with much smaller bodies, and she usually never hesitated to do what she wanted to, but today, for some reason, she had hesitated to ride the horses. But now, as she entered the stables and saw the fine animals and smelled their scent, an old, familiar excitement began to rise up inside her.

She went directly to a beautiful red stallion with fire in his eyes. She forgot about Mike as she gently rubbed the stallion's soft nose and mouth.

The horse responded by moving closer and nudging his muzzle into Julia's caressing hand. She was smiling and talking quietly to the horse when she became aware of Mike close beside her.

"Something's not quite right here," he commented softly.

"What do you mean?" she asked, looking up at him.

"You're obviously not only a horse lover, you have a definite knack with them."

"Why do you say that?"

"Because I've never seen Big Red react to any human being like this before. And he's quite definitely responding to you." He sounded puzzled.

"Why do you keep him if he doesn't like people?"

"Because the female horses like to make babies with him." The amusement was creeping back into his voice. "Now, confess. You're not a stranger to horses, are you?"

"Okay. I grew up on a horse ranch in Texas. I lived on a horse from the time I was three years old until I left home ten years ago. But I haven't been back on one since then and I was afraid I couldn't handle myself like I used to, and I knew how disappointed that would have made me."

"Would you like to try?"

"Yes! I want to ride him!" She indicated the red stallion.

"No!"

"Yes! Yes, I want to ride Big Red." She felt excitement growing inside her at the thought of being part of the power this beautiful animal emanated.

"No, Julia!" The firm authority in Mike's voice shot a thrill through her, and at the same time challenged her.

He had moved closer, and although his voice was firm and hard, his eyes were soft and gentle as he locked gazes with her.

She couldn't pull her eyes away from his intent stare as he continued, "I've only just met you, but I can't stand the thought of you getting hurt."

She sensed he was going to kiss her, and she knew she was going to let him, when Big Red stuck his nose between them to nuzzle her again.

They both laughed, the spell broken, and Julia reached out again to caress the big animal.

"Come on," Mike said, taking her arm, "let's go saddle Dilly and Dally. They're good for an old pro who hasn't ridden in a while."

Deciding that it was probably a better idea not to argue with him at this point, she followed him to where two beautiful speckled gray horses with huge, soft eyes watched them approach.

Mike began saddling the two mares, who, according to him, were the only twin horses in the county. Julia helped him, realizing how much she'd missed horses and how little she'd forgotten. As they finished saddling the animals, without even thinking she stepped in the stirrup and swung herself into the saddle.

Only when she was settled into the saddle did she realize what she'd done. Mike stood watching her with an admiring look on his face.

"Well, you comin' or not, Pardner?" she drawled, a gleam of excitement flashing in her eyes.

The look he gave her held something more than amusement now, but Julia didn't take time to analyze it as she guided her horse down the trail and felt the old familiar feeling of freedom that always engulfed her when she was on the back of a horse.

The leaves were blazing with fall colors, and the breeze touching her face had the promise of winter in it. Julia found herself wondering how it would be to spend a winter with Mike.

She was startled when he said from beside her, "A penny for your thoughts."

"My thoughts are worth more than a penny, sir!" she answered, with a haughty tilt of her chin.

But instead of the chuckle and typical reaction she expected from him, he just watched her with such intensity that she unexpectedly felt a wave of shyness wash over her.

"What?" she asked. Her large blue eyes sparkled and her auburn hair blew gently in the breeze.

"You're beautiful, you know that?"

Normally, Julia would have laughed and made some flippant remark, but the seriousness in his eyes gave no room for joking.

"Thank you," she said, looking away from him briefly, only to look back again.

The power of his gaze made her pulse race wildly, and her entire body seemed to be turning to molten lava.

They came to a widening of the trail, and Mike stopped his horse and got off. He came around to Julia's side and reached up for her. "Come here."

She put her hands on his shoulders and let him pull her off her horse.

As her feet touched the ground, his mouth claimed hers. Julia had been kissed many times before, but never had she felt such an intoxicating draining of her very soul.

Slowly, and very gently, Mike pulled away from her lips, but kept his arms around her waist.

"Do you always kiss strangers this thoroughly?" she asked weakly, trying to regain her composure. "Is this part of everyone's trail ride?"

"It's been a long time since I've seen a woman that I wanted to kiss at all," he answered, gazing deeply into her eyes "but that's all I've been able to think about since I saw you this morning."

He stepped away from Julia to untangle the reins from one of the horses' hooves. He handed the reins to her, picked up his own, and started to walk down the trail.

Julia walked beside him, not interrupting the quiet moment. After a few minutes, Mike stopped and turned to her.

"Julia, stay here this winter. Wait," he said, as he sensed she was about to stop him. "Hear me out. Stay here. I own this resort. Give us a chance to get to know each other. I know it's too early to judge a relationship, but as I said, it's been a long, long time since I've seen a woman I felt this attracted to. If you leave now, we won't have a chance to find out if anything can come of this obvious attraction we have for each other."

"We could write." Julia's half-hearted argument fell on deaf ears.

"I don't want to write. I want to be with you, to see you, to feel you—" Again his arms were around her.

"Wait!" Julia's hands against his chest stopped the kiss. "What about my job?" she tried to reason again.

"Get a leave of absence." He pulled her closer. "With your knowledge of horses, you can work here at the resort. We can spend our days working together and getting to know each other."

"But what about—" She could feel her strength weakening as he continued to press her toward him.

"Just one winter, Julia. Just a few months to see if we want to spend our lives together." His strength was too much for her to resist and she felt herself being crushed in his arms again. This time the kiss was gentle and probing and persuading.

And Julia knew winter would be beautiful, with snow on the mountains, and a fire in the fireplace, and—

A Walk in the Park

I—hate—jog—ging. I—hate—jog—ging. My thoughts keep rhythm with my feet as I do my morning routine of jogging through the little park close to my apartment.

I'm really proud of myself for staying with my new exercise program for so long this time. It's been two solid weeks since I started. That's the longest I've ever lasted! No more stupid diets, I've promised myself, but I will make an effort to stay healthy through eating right and exercising. I can handle the eating right—most of the time—but I do hate to exercise! Especially this damn jogging.

There he is. Every morning I meet him at the same place. He's walking his Great Dane—or the dog is walking him. Sometimes it's hard to tell which. Most of the time we speak, that is, if the dog doesn't strike off on a side trip just as we get close to each other. Every day I find myself watching for him and his dog. It takes my mind off my misery.

I wonder if he's married. If he—

"What the—?" I hear him exclaim, just as I see a cat running across the trail in front of us. The dog sees the cat at the same time and leaps for it, dragging her master with her. The cat gets away, but by now the dog's leash is wrapped around my feet, and I feel myself falling. I try to brace my fall, but only succeed in catching most of my weight on my right hand. Pain shoots up my arm like a piercing flame.

The dog immediately starts licking my face—like that's going to make up for the accident it just caused. I try to ward off the big dog with my left hand and sit up, but I can't push myself up with my hurt hand, so I just moan and lie back down on the cool grass, and try to protect my face from the long, wet tongue that seems to be everywhere at once.

"Madame X! Stay!" his voice commands the big Great Dane, and immediately the licking stops.

"Are you hurt?" I realize his question is for me, so I slowly uncover my damp face and look up at the man kneeling beside me.

"I don't know," I answer, trying to sit up. "I fell on my hand, and it hurts pretty bad." I hold my hand out to look at it, and we both gasp at the same time. It's already swelling and turning blue.

"We'd better get you to a doctor," he says, as he reaches out and takes my swollen hand in his. His large hands gently inspect my bruised one.

"I really don't think it's broken," I assure him. "I think it'll be fine if I just go home and put some ice on it."

"Can you move your fingers?" I make my best effort at moving my fingers, but they barely move before the pain causes me to groan.

"Cindy, we have to get you to the doctor." He's standing now, and helping me to my feet.

"No. I'm going home and try the ice first. I can't afford an emergency room trip, unless I have to."

"Look, my dog caused this accident, so I'll pay all expenses," he insists.

"I'm going home, now," I state determinedly, and start walking back to my apartment.

"Then I'm coming with you to help you get an ice pack. You can't manage very well with just one hand. And besides that, your apartment's on the third floor. I'm going to make sure you get there safely."

By now my arm's hurting too badly to argue with him. I can only concentrate on getting home and sitting down with a cold pack on my hand and arm.

I try to unlock my door with my left hand, but can't get the key in the lock.

"Here, let me," he says, taking the key from me.

At this point sanity overrules my pain, and I realize a complete stranger is about to enter my apartment with me.

"What's your name?" I ask.

"Stan Johnson. I promise you I'm not a criminal on the loose. Would I have a lovely dog like this, that I walk every day, if I wasn't on the up and up?"

I like the twinkle in his soft brown eyes. And he does seem harmless. He seems quite nice, actually. "Okay, Stan Johnson. Since you refuse to believe I'm okay, I guess you can come in and help me put ice on my hand." By now, the pain is taking over my thoughts again.

Stan takes control of the situation, and before I know what's happening I'm lying on my couch with an ice pack neatly tucked around my swollen hand and arm. He's also given me two nonprescription pain pills and a glass of water.

"Now you leave that ice on there for at least two hours. If it isn't feeling better after a couple of hours, I'm taking you to the emergency room to get X-rays. You might have a slight fracture, even if it isn't broken. Agreed?"

"Agreed," I mumble, just wanting to be alone to suffer in peace.

"Okay. I'll call you in two hours. If you aren't better, I'll take you to the doctor," he says, walking out the door and locking it behind him.

I come slowly awake to the shrill ringing of the phone. I automatically reach for it with my right hand, only to be reminded of my situation by the ice pack that's still wrapped around it and my right arm. By the time I change positions and reach for the phone with my left hand, the caller hangs up.

Now I'm fully awake, and I realize I don't have any pain in my hand. I quickly unwrap the ice pack and am overjoyed to find the swelling has actually gone down some, and I can move my fingers freely.

My first impulse is to call Stan and tell him the good news. But I don't know his phone number. That's when I remember he said he would call me. But how does he know my number? And, in fact, how did he know my name? And how did he know that I live on the third floor of an apartment building? And how did he lock my door when he left?

He took my key! Now my heart is pounding. This seems too strange. Who is this Stan Johnson? Has he been stalking me? He knows my name, he knows where I live, and now he has a key to my apartment! Yet the only place I've ever seen him is walking his dog in the park.

How could I have been so irresponsible? My parents would have a fit if they knew how stupid I've acted!

The knock on the door startles me. Is it Stan? He said he'd call first. Was that him calling earlier? No, that couldn't be. He couldn't get here that fast.

I go to the door and look through the peephole to see Stan standing there as if he's trying to look back at me. He must have heard me come to the door, because he's smiling and waving. He really is a handsome man, but my new suspicions have me afraid to open the door, so, slipping the safety chain in place, I just crack it slightly.

"I'm okay now. See?" I try to show him my hand through the crack. "The swelling is almost all gone. But thanks for checking, anyway. And thanks for taking care of me. If you'll just give me back my door key, you can go on home."

"What's going on? Why are you acting so strange? Look." He's holding up an envelope. "I want to give you this. I was going to give it to you this morning, but when Madame X caused you to fall, I forgot about it."

"What is it?" I ask, trying to see the writing on the envelope.

"Nope. You aren't going to see it until you let me in," Stan says, putting the envelope behind his back, a teasing look playing in his eyes.

"I thought you were going to call before you came."

"I did call, and you didn't answer. That worried me, so I came to check on you."

"How did you get here that fast?"

"No more answers until you open the door." From the big grin on his face, he seems to be enjoying our little game.

I'm beginning to feel silly talking through the crack in the door, so I unchain it and step back. I'm sure my next-door neighbor is home and can hear me scream if Stan tries anything weird. "Let me see the envelope."

"Let me see your hand, first."

I hold my hand out and wriggle my fingers as if nothing had ever happened.

"That's great!" Stan seems genuinely pleased. "Okay, here's your envelope." He hands me the envelope, and it's addressed to me, at apartment #214.

"Someone put the wrong address on this." I'm talking to myself, more than to Stan. "My apartment is #314. But how did you get it?"

"My apartment is #214," he says.

"But how did you know this was mine?" I still can't figure it out.

"My apartment is directly under yours. I saw you the day you moved in, and I see you often as you come and go. I started walking Madame X at the same time you jog, hoping I could meet you. But I really didn't mean for it to happen like this."

"Do you just sit at your window and spy on me?"

"I'm a freelance writer. If you read the morning paper, you'd be familiar with my column, and my picture. I work at home and my desk is beside the window. I see everyone who passes by, but I enjoy watching some more than others." That wicked little grin is back.

"Do you like to jog?" His question comes while I'm still admiring his grin.

"No. I hate it." I can't tell a lie.

"Then why don't you start walking with Madame X and me? The

experts are saying now that walking is just as good as jogging. Madame X really likes you, and I'm sure she'd love to have you accompany us each morning."

I hesitate, still unsure of his motives, although he seems wonderfully sincere. Tomorrow I'll buy a morning paper, and check out his column.

"Okay, if you can keep her from around my ankles," I agree.

His smile spreads across his face.

Suddenly, exercise has become something I'm looking forward to.

The Company Party

Shanna stared at the door that had just slammed closed, disbelief apparent on her face. Who the hell did Tom think he was to talk like that to her?

They'd dated for months and he had never said anything about her weight. In fact, it had never seemed to bother him. He'd never even seemed to notice she carried some extra pounds. So for that reason, she'd assumed he loved her just the way she was. After all, *he* was the one who had approached *her* and asked her out, initially.

But now, tonight, he'd dropped this bombshell.

The company he worked for was having their annual employee party in two weeks, and he'd asked her if she could lose some weight before they went. She'd stared at him a full sixty seconds before telling him to go straight to hell. He'd just shaken his head and walked out the door.

Shanna reached for the phone and dialed a number. "Louise? What are you doing tonight? Okay, I'll be over there in one hour. We're going out for a while."

She'd show that arrogant bastard.

Two hours later found Shanna and Louise, her best friend, in Tanner's Place. The house band was good here, and Shanna needed to hear some music and dance a little. She needed to get in a better mood.

They sat at a corner table and ordered a couple of drinks, then just relaxed and listened to the music and watched the couples on the dance floor.

Shanna's eyes rested on one couple in particular. The man danced with his eyes half closed, and she couldn't quite read his expression. But the woman he danced with was flirting with any man who would look her way.

The man intrigued Shanna. His dark hair was thick and slightly wavy. Perfect for running fingers through. His white tuxedo shirt was open at the neck, allowing a V of dark chest hair to spiral out. The sleeves of his shirt were rolled back a couple of folds and the same dark hair curled on his forearms.

A small tingling of awareness and excitement started fluttering in the pit of Shanna's stomach. She wanted to meet this man. She wanted to feel those arms holding her while they danced. She wanted to lay her cheek on his shoulder just close enough to feel the pulse at the base of his throat, and she wanted to kiss him on that same spot.

Neither the man nor the woman wore wedding rings, so Shanna hoped that meant they weren't married. But she knew she had to find out. She wouldn't leave tonight without knowing his marital status.

"Shanna, what on earth are you staring at?" Louise's voice brought Shanna reluctantly back to the moment.

"That beautiful man over there who's dancing with that inattentive woman." She guided her friend's attention to the couple.

"Don't you know who that is?" Louise asked in surprise.

"No," Shanna answered, getting out of her chair, "but I'm going to find out. I'm going to ask him to dance." Her mind was made up, and she didn't see any reason to wait any longer.

"Shanna! Wait!" But the music drowned out Louise's protests.

Shanna tapped the woman on the shoulder and asked, "May I cut in?"

As the startled woman looked at Shanna with her mouth open to protest, the man said, "You sure may!" His voice was smooth and sensual, and made a tiny thrill creep up Shanna's spine. His warm, light-brown eyes gazed down at her.

"Hi, I'm Shanna," she said as he slid his arms around her and guided her into step with the music.

"I'm John," he returned. "Thank you for rescuing me."

"Is she your wife?"

"She used to be. We've been divorced for three years. She couldn't remember whose bed she was supposed to be in at night."

"She's crazy!" Shanna loved the way he smiled down at her. His eyes were open now, unlike when he danced with his ex-wife. And they devoured Shanna.

"You're beautiful! Don't tell me you're here alone."

"Thanks, and yes, I'm here alone," she answered, snuggling closer to his warm chest. "Well, I'm here with a friend, but she's having her own fun."

"Well, I think I can remedy that situation," he promised, pulling her closer.

Shanna rested her head on his shoulder in that special spot and tenderly smiled as she felt his pounding pulse. She felt him lay his cheek on her hair and softly sigh, his strong arms gathering her as close to him as he could.

And they danced.

And they danced.

And they danced.

Even when the band finished one song and started another one, they continued to dance. Finally, Louise tapped Shanna on the shoulder and said, "Everyone's gone home except us. Can we leave now?"

John asked Shanna, "May I call you tomorrow?"

Shanna smiled and said, "Please do."

In the car, Louise repeated her previous question. "Do you know who that is?"

"That's John," Shanna said with a schoolgirl giggle. "And he's going to call me tomorrow."

"That's the owner of the company where Tom works! That's Tom's boss!" Louise said emphatically.

"Well, won't Tom be surprised when I show up at the company party with his boss?" Shanna smiled.

A Weakness for Candy

Candi chose her favorite table in the corner of the courtyard of the little café just around the corner from the antique shop where she worked. Arranging her lunch around her, she sat down and breathed a sigh of relaxation. She loved the hour she spent here each day. The table sat very close to the street, but a clump of honeysuckle vine covered the fence and shielded her from the view of any passersby, giving her the illusion that she was alone in her own little world.

"What is that?" A high-pitched, accusing woman's voice just the other side of the honeysuckle vine startled Candi out of her relaxed calm.

"Well, I believe it's called a candy bar," replied a man's voice. A voice that was so deep it could have been doing the bass lead in a gospel quartet.

"And why are you eating it?" Again, the accusation in the woman's voice carried condemnation.

"Because it's noon, and I'm hungry?" The man's voice remained calm and undisturbed.

"I thought we'd discussed your eating habits, Kane."

Candi was overcome now with curiosity. She shifted in her chair until she found a small opening in the honeysuckle vine that allowed her to peek through and see the couple standing on the street very close to her. The woman, a tall, thin blonde, stood with both hands on her hips, glaring at the man. A giant of a man. He had to be at least six feet four inches tall. And he had to weigh close to 400 pounds, Candi decided. He was thick. Solid. Wide shoulders, huge, well-shaped arms and legs, and, while his stomach protruded some, it wasn't out of proportion to the rest of his body. He looked like he could be a star player on any football team.

"No, Hazel, *you* discussed my eating habits." His slightly sarcastic smile revealed beautiful white teeth that gleamed under his dark mustache. But the smile didn't reach his smoky blue eyes. Beautiful eyes, Candi noted.

He raked a huge hand through his mass of thick black hair and said resignedly, "I told you that I eat one candy bar a day. Now if I were a thin man, you'd laugh it off and say I needed the candy bar for energy. But since I'm a fat man, you think I'm eating it because I can't help myself. I believe that was *my* part of the discussion about food."

"But why do you have to eat *any* candy? Why can't you just eat healthy food?" the high-pitched voice persisted, growing more piercing.

"Number one, I'm not going to try and live on rabbit food. I can't do my job when all I have to eat is lettuce and tomatoes. And, number two, I have a weakness for candy, so I allow myself a bar a day. If that's going to cut a couple of years off my life, so be it. At least I'll be happy the years I do live."

"So you just refuse to try and lose that weight. Is that what you're telling me?"

"Hazel, you know all of my family are large. It's a family trait. You've met them all." He plopped the last part of the candy bar into his mouth and deliberately savored it until it was gone.

"Yes, and I've seen how much they eat, too." Contempt sounded in every word.

"Actually, they don't eat any more than you do. Hazel, you can put that food away!" This time his laugh was genuine and rumbled from the massive chest.

"But I'm not fat. I'm one of those people who don't have to worry about that."

"So? What does that have to do with anything? Do you think you're a walking good-health ad just because you're thin? People *are* what they eat. It doesn't matter what size they are. And just because a person's thin doesn't automatically make them healthy."

Candi, a plus-size woman herself, wanted to get up and go hug this mountain of a man.

"I've heard your soap-box speeches before, so spare me. Bottom line is, are you going to lose weight, or are we going to have to call it quits?"

"Well, Hazel, I've done a lot of thinking about this, and I guess it's just time we kissed and said good-bye." He lapsed into singing the old rock song.

"You're serious, aren't you? You'd rather hang on to some weakness for candy than keep me!" Disbelief sounded in her squeaky voice. "Well, I'm glad I found this out before we took this relationship any further!" She stormed down the street, leaving the big man staring after her.

"Yeah, me too," he mumbled, again raking his hand through his hair, and trying to hide the flash of pain that crossed his face.

Suddenly Candi, who wasn't an impulsive person at all, acted on impulse.

"Kane?" she called through the honeysuckle vine.

"What the—?" The big man peered at the vine, trying to see who'd called his name. Then, turning, he walked the few steps that brought him around the corner of the fence and spotted Candi sitting in her corner, her mass of golden-red hair blowing in the breeze and a smile gleaming in her big green eyes.

"You heard the entire conversation, didn't you?" he said, looking slightly embarrassed.

"Yes, I'm afraid I did. Would you like to join me for lunch?" She slid a chair out for him.

"Sure!" he agreed, sitting down. "What's your name?"

"Candi," she answered, with a smile that melted all the hurt from his big heart.

Mail Order Bribe

Shannon O'Shay's legs almost buckled under her as she stepped from the Greyhound bus onto the wet street. Partly because of the long drive from Salt Lake City, but mostly from fear.

As the rain that ran down the street like a tiny river threatened to creep over the top of her lace-up shoes, she cursed the events that brought her to the small mining town of Clear Springs, Utah. Cursed the disease that threatened her dad's life to the point that she had to sell her very soul to make sure he was taken care of. Cursed the genes that allowed her to fit the description—how had her dad told her the ad read? *Wanted: A large, sturdy woman young enough to bear children, and strong enough to stand the rugged Utah winters.* Cursed the—

"Miss Shannon O'Shay?"

Shannon slowly swiveled her head to look at the owner of the voice and realized her worst fears. He was probably forty years her senior. Some old miner who realized time was running out and decided he wanted a child to bear his name and a woman to take care of him in his old age. At least, she reasoned, maybe he'd only have the energy to "do it" just enough to get her pregnant, then he'd leave her alone. The thought brought a slight smile to her face as she answered him.

"Yes, I'm Shannon O'Shay."

"Ah, but you're beautiful! The description in your letter didn't do you justice." His voice was young and energetic in spite of his years.

"Since my dad was the one who wrote the letter, I wouldn't know," Shannon answered.

"Well, he said you had red hair. He should have said you had hair that flashed like burnt gold in the sunlight. He said you had green eyes. He should have said your eyes are the color of fresh young leaves in the early spring, after a thunderstorm. He said you had a good childbearing body. He should have said you have wonderful childbearing hips, which taper in at the waist to give accent to your full, lovely breasts. He said—"

"Sir?" Shannon's face was glowing red by now. "Sir, he's my father. I don't think he'd write something like that about me."

"I'm sorry. I've embarrassed you. Come on, let's go home."

Home. Home was Salt Lake City, and, Shannon realized as she allowed this stranger to aid her in stepping up into a beat-up old pickup truck, it would be a long time before she could go home. Maybe never. Reality, heavy and cold, settled in the pit of her stomach.

The suitcase, with what clothes she could pack in it, was heaved onto the back of the pickup by a young man who'd volunteered the kind service.

"My name's Jack Riley." The stranger interrupted her sad thoughts as he climbed into the seat beside her. "My place is about ten miles from here. The house ain't that grand, but it ain't too bad, either. It's warm enough in the winter, if that eases some of your fears. Since fall is about on us, I thought maybe you might want to know that."

As he talked, Shannon saw remnants of a handsome young man. His eyes were brown and warm. They didn't seem like the eyes of a cruel man. That had been one of her greatest fears. That she was going into a situation where the man would be cruel and demanding.

"That was actually one of my least worries," she answered him honestly.

"What was your greatest worry?" he asked, keeping his eyes on the deep ruts that led through the never-ending mud that she assumed was supposed to be a road.

"That you'd be cruel and mean." She was almost afraid just uttering the words would activate the attitude in him.

"Yes, I can understand why that would be a fear for a woman coming into this kind of situation," he agreed, glancing briefly at her before continuing. "But I can assure you that I'm not mean or cruel. You don't have to worry about that."

The rest of the ride was fairly quiet, with Jack Riley commenting briefly on anything he thought might be of interest as they passed.

Although the truck ride was much more uncomfortable than the bus had been, Shannon leaned back and tried to relax. Up until she'd gotten on the bus this morning, her thoughts and energy had gone into trying to figure out a way to earn enough money so she didn't have to leave the home and city she loved.

She'd been born in Salt Lake City. Had lived there all of her life. And it had been a happy, carefree life until her mom died five years ago. After that, her dad had gone downhill. She even suspected that he'd developed a gambling problem and had lost a good bit of money.

But none of the better paying jobs had worked out for her. It was almost as if the strong force of fate was pulling her along into this new situation.

Her dad had been diagnosed with a rare lung disease, with a name she couldn't even try to pronounce, and had to have special treatment that cost much more than they could afford. Then the letter had come. A letter offering more than enough money for the doctor bills, if Shannon would agree to be the wife of a stranger. Her dad had jumped at the chance to get the treatment he needed. He'd been vague about the origin and contents of the letter, except the part about the kind of woman this person was looking for.

When she'd asked him how the person who sent the letter knew they needed money, her father assured her that was just coincidence.

"Come on, old girl, you can do it! Pull this one last hill and your work will be done for the day," Jack told the old truck as he maneuvered it through an arched gateway that simply read "Riley" and headed up a steep incline.

As they topped the knoll, Jack stopped the truck, and Shannon's breath caught in her throat. The scene that lay in the valley below her was nothing she could have imagined. The ranch house was a huge, rambling white structure with a porch that encircled it. Bunkhouses and a massive barn sat a respectful distance from the main house. To the left of the structures was a luxuriant pasture with cows milling around, grazing on the fertile green grass. Cowboys scurried about doing chores they had been assigned. This was definitely not a mining camp.

"Surprised?" Jack Riley had been watching her expression.

"Very," Shannon said, and smiled at him for the first time, as relief flooded her.

"And your dad's letter didn't mention that you had a smile that could melt the coldest heart in the deepest dead of winter."

"Thank you, Mr. Riley," Shannon said. "Thank you for all your compliments to me this day."

"Aw, now, we can't have any of that 'Mr. Riley' stuff. If we're going to be living in the same house, you need to call me Jack, okay?"

"Okay," she reluctantly muttered, again feeling apprehension at the thought of sharing the house with this stranger.

"Okay!" Jack declared and guided the truck on down the hill.

After telling one of the cowboys to put Shannon's luggage in the "upper bedroom facing the east pasture," Jack Riley led her up the doorsteps onto the huge porch.

She glanced around at the comfortable rockers lining the porch and could imagine sitting out here at night, relaxing after a long day's work.

The screen door squeaked as Jack swung it open for Shannon to precede him through it.

"Molly, we're home," he called.

They stood in a big parlor, with what Shannon considered amazingly modern furniture. It was all coming as a great surprise to her, since she'd been expecting to be carried to a miner's shack with little more than a roof and the roughest of necessities.

A short, petite woman came bustling through the doors, wiping her hands on a floral apron tied around her waist.

She stopped short when she spotted Shannon. "Oh, my!" she breathed, barely above a whisper. "You're him made over."

"Molly!" Jack scolded in a warning voice.

"She's so beautiful, Jack," Molly said, coming closer to Shannon, as if to get a better look at her.

Molly looked to be about Jack's age. Maybe a little younger. Her face, though beginning to show the signs of age, still held a youthful beauty. Shannon knew she must have been a beautiful young woman.

Molly reached up and gently touched Shannon's face. "Welcome to our home, Shannon O'Shay," she said. Shannon sensed tears were just beneath the surface of the woman's sky-blue eyes.

What a strange welcome, Shannon thought a few moments later, when she was left alone in the huge bedroom she'd been assigned to. Who was Molly? Shannon got the feeling there was more between Jack and Molly than rancher and housekeeper, or whatever Molly was. There was a connection between them. And Molly acted as if she knew Shannon. Or, at least, knew *of* her.

This day was not turning out as Shannon had expected at all. Still uncertain of her future, she couldn't help but feel relief settling over her. Her situation didn't seem nearly as bad as it had this morning when she left Salt Lake City.

She sat down on the side of the four-poster bed and gently ran her hands over the handmade quilt adorning it. How beautiful it was. Bright, happy colors had been pieced together carefully. Meticulous, tiny stitches held the material together with love. *Did Molly make it?* she wondered.

The room was large, with a fireplace on the far wall and a rocking chair placed at an angle in front of it. A rocking chair. To rock the baby she was supposed to give to Jack Riley? Reality came back to

Shannon O'Shay with full force. She was here to become the wife of someone and give him an heir.

Before fear could set in she went to the adjoining bathroom and splashed water on her hands, arms and face. Molly had told her to freshen up and come back downstairs. The evening meal would be served in thirty minutes.

Glancing in the ornate oval mirror that hung over the sink, Shannon fluffed her hair and smoothed over her eyebrows. She glanced around the bathroom. What a relief to know she'd have her own bathroom and wouldn't have to share it with anyone.

Dreading to go back downstairs, she headed for the door. Before closing it, she turned and looked back at the bedroom. It would be a comfortable room. And she knew she would need a lot of comfort in the coming months.

She was halfway down the carved oak staircase when she heard angry voices. Stunned, she stopped, without thinking, to listen to what was being said.

"Dad, what have you done?" The voice was deep and vibrant and very angry.

"Now, Son, before you jump to any conclusions—"

So Jack already had a son? Then why did he need a wife to bear him another one?

"I'm not jumping to conclusions, Dad. You know this isn't the first time you've tried to get me married off to someone! But it's the first time you've brought them into the house! That's even worse!"

The truth dawned on Shannon, hard and cold. She wasn't brought here for Jack Riley. She was brought here for his son. Abruptly, she was thrown right back into the dilemma that she'd started from. She'd allowed herself to relax too soon.

Overwhelmed with the new knowledge, she wanted to turn and run back to the warm, quiet room she'd just left. But she couldn't. She knew she had to face her future sooner or later, so she might as well get it over with.

On shaking legs, she proceeded toward the voices, hoping she would somehow disappear into thin air before she had to go through the huge double doors that she was sure led to the dining room.

Molly walked past the door and saw Shannon approaching.

"Here she comes, now," she chirped cheerfully. Shannon knew she was warning the two arguing men.

"Come on in here," Molly said, taking Shannon's hand. "We have someone we want you to meet. This is John, Jack's son."

The two men stood facing each other, angry eyes locked in battle.

John Riley was a striking man. Where his dad was medium height, John was well over six feet tall. Where his dad had gray hair and warm brown eyes, John had dark brown hair and cold, steel-gray eyes. Hard. Piercing. Angry eyes that caught and held Shannon's only briefly before skirting down her body, then back to her face.

"Well, Dad, you really outdid yourself this time. You found the opposite of Lisa, didn't you? Is that supposed to help me forget her?" Sarcasm scorched the air around him.

"Son, Lisa's—" Jack started.

"Don't!" John's sharp voice interrupted him. "Do not speak that word into the air, Dad."

"Okay, boys, that's enough!" Molly's voice turned both heads toward her. "We're going to eat supper now, and we're not going to argue the entire meal. This subject isn't going anywhere any time soon, so it can rest for awhile."

"You're right, Mol," Jack said, pulling out a chair and sitting down at the head of the table.

John yanked out a chair and sat down. Molly indicated a seat for Shannon to sit, and took a chair close to Jack.

Shannon hadn't realized how hungry she was until the scent of the food wafted up as she took each bowl handed to her and placed the food on her plate.

As John handed her the plate of cornbread, she accidentally touched his hand when she took the plate. She jerked her hand away as if burned when awareness, sharp and vivid, shot up her arm. The plate would have fallen if he hadn't still had a good hold on it.

"Sorry," she muttered, and reached back for the waiting plate of cornbread. She thought she saw a glimpse of amusement cross his handsome features, but it didn't last long enough for her to be sure.

"Dad, how is this woman supposed to give you grandchildren if she jumps like she's been shot and apologizes when our hands barely touch? If you were going to go to the trouble of mail ordering me a bride, surely you could have found me a warm, loving, experienced one. Not one who's trying to act like a virgin."

"John Riley! What's come over you? You don't usually act like such a cad." Molly's voice was sharp and reproachful.

"Maybe I should have taken my meal in the bunkhouse with the guys tonight," John said. "If anyone had warned me of the situation, that's what I would have done."

"Well, it ain't too late, Son," Jack said coldly. "You're making a real ass of yourself."

At his father's statement, John stood abruptly and left the house. The screen door slammed loudly behind him.

"Maybe we should have told him what we were doing," Molly said.

"No. If we had, he'd have done everything in his power to keep us from bringing Shannon here."

Shannon stared at her plate of untouched food while the two talked about her as if she weren't sitting there.

"Shannon, I'm sorry you had to witness this argument tonight. I know you're tired from your long day. Eat your food and go get a good night's sleep. This will settle down tomorrow." Jack's voice was not as reassuring as he'd hoped it would be.

But once Shannon started eating the wonderful peas, corn, fried okra and cornbread, she did begin to feel better. Maybe things *would* settle down tomorrow.

Two months had passed since Shannon had come to the Riley ranch. During that time, she'd learned in bits and pieces that Molly was Jack's second wife. He'd been married briefly before her, and John was his son by the first marriage. She didn't know what had happened to John's mother, but apparently Molly and Jack had married when John was a very small boy, and he thought of Molly as his mother. John was thirty-seven. Ten years her senior.

But nothing was said to her about trying to get the two of them married. And nothing was said about how long she would stay here under the circumstances. It was a very strange situation that she didn't understand. But she didn't see any reason to question it. She didn't have anywhere else to go.

She'd written her father, but hadn't heard anything back. Would she even know about it if he died? The thought made her sad, but she was still angry with him for allowing her to be in this situation. If he hadn't squandered his retirement fund he'd have had enough money to take care of himself, and she wouldn't have to sacrifice her happiness for him.

Sure, she knew she had a choice. She could just pack her bags and disappear. But to where? She wasn't one of those brave-hearted women who could move into any city and start a life on her own. And her father was all the family she had left. She couldn't turn her back on him, no matter how much he deserved it.

She learned that John had been married to Lisa, but Lisa had died, alone, one night when their baby tried to come into the world prematurely. Some of the things Jack had said the first day they met made more sense to Shannon now.

The way John reacted to her arrival also made more sense. It was clear Jack and Molly wanted John to be happy. To have a wife and children. And it was clear that John wasn't interested in finding a wife and trying to have children. That's why he was so miserable. He'd tried that and it hadn't worked. He was probably afraid to fall in love again and try to have a child, if the truth were known.

Such were the thoughts flying around in Shannon's head as she hung a load of laundry on the line to dry. The dryer had quit and the broken part had to be ordered, so she and Molly were line-drying the clothes.

It was September and a strong fall breeze popped the clothes that she'd already hung. They would be dry soon in this wind. Just as she tried to maneuver a sheet to the line, a gust caught it and plopped it back over her head and body. She frantically tried to extricate herself from the wet sheet without letting any of it touch the ground.

Suddenly she was aware of someone helping her get the sheet off of her head. When her face was finally clear she found herself looking straight into the glint of steel gray eyes.

John threw the sheet over the line and turned back to Shannon. She was trying to brush the hair back out of her face when two strong hands caught her wrists and stopped her in mid-stroke.

"Leave it. The wind will just mess it up again. Do you have any idea how beautiful your hair is in the sunlight?"

Too surprised to speak, Shannon just stared at John. After all this time of ignoring her at every turn, of skipping meals with the family because she was there, after shooting snide remarks at her every chance he got, he was now paying her a compliment? And not just a compliment. There was warmth in his voice that she'd never heard before. A spark in those eyes that held something other than contempt.

"Do you have any idea how your green eyes glint when you're angry at something I've said? Do you have any idea how kissable those bow-shaped lips of yours are? And do you have any possible idea how much I want to touch your full, rounded breasts?"

Before she could think of anything to say, John placed his hands on each side of her waist and pulled her hard against him, capturing her lips in a soft, sensual kiss. Only then did she smell the alcohol. He'd been drinking! That's why he was saying those things to her!

"Shannon, are you about ready for another load of clothes to hang up?" Molly called from the shed where the washer and dryer were.

"We'll carry this conversation on later," John promised, and reluctantly backed away from her.

"Almost," Shannon called to Molly in a shaky voice, and finished pinning the sheet to the line.

She held onto the clothesline for a few moments to steady her shaking legs. Her lips still throbbed from the kiss. Throbbed for more. The yearning that she'd been fighting took root deep inside her heart.

Even as intolerable as John had been to her, she knew she was attracted to him. The thought of marrying him and sharing his bed wasn't that repulsive, at all. In fact, sometimes at night—most nights, if she wanted to be honest with herself—she'd lie in her bed and wonder how it would be to be married to him. To be his wife. Now, after that kiss—

Shaking herself back to reality, Shannon tried to get her mind on what she was supposed to be doing. Should she tell Molly what had just happened? Or let it go? She was sure after the alcohol wore off John would be back to his old self, and probably wouldn't even remember what he'd said.No. She'd just let it drop. No use in causing more tension.

But later that day as she and Molly prepared supper, Molly said, "Today's the anniversary of Lisa's death. It's always a hard day for John. He probably won't come down tonight. He usually stays in his room and gets drunk."

Well, he's already started that, Shannon thought. But she was relieved Molly didn't think he'd come downstairs to supper tonight. She really didn't want to face him after the way her body had reacted to his touch today. Did he know how he'd affected her? Had he felt her heartbeat jump rhythm and pound in her chest?

But her luck didn't hold. Just as they sat down to eat, John walked into the room. He had on clean jeans, a light blue shirt that emphasized his eyes, and his boots had been polished to a spit-shine.

"Are you going out, Son?" Jack asked. Even when he was displeased with his son, his voice held special warmth when he spoke to him. Tonight, pride shone in Jack Riley's eyes as he looked at his handsome son.

"Yes, I think I'll ride into town and see if anything's happening. Would you like to go?" He startled everyone in the room by directing his question to Shannon.

"Oh! I—uh—I would have to clean up. I've been working all day in these clothes," she managed to say.

"You look great to me," he answered. "Come just like you are. Nobody will know you've been doing chores all day. We'll finish supper, then ride in and look around. Some of the boys said a new country band was in town. We can go see how they sound."

Should she mention to anyone that he'd been drinking? Was he still drinking? Was that why he was suddenly being so nice to her? And why weren't Jack and Molly questioning him about this if they knew it was his nature to get drunk on this night every year?

As if reading her mind, Jack quietly spoke. "John, are you in any position to drive?"

"Yes, Dad. I did have a few drinks this afternoon," he said, glancing sheepishly at Shannon, "but I decided that the headache that I'll have in the morning just isn't worth it."

"So will you come with me?" He repeated his invitation to Shannon.

"Of course, she'll go with you, Son. She needs to get out of this house for a while. She's used to being in the big city, so she's probably bored to death here." Jack made the decision for her. And why not? She was here, after all, to marry his son, wasn't she?

"You kids sit down and eat, now, before you rush off," Molly chimed in. A smile beamed on her face.

Too nervous to eat, Shannon excused herself and went to her room to change her clothes. She didn't care what John said; she wasn't going to town in clothes she'd worked in all day.

After taking a quick shower, she put on a dress she hadn't worn since she'd been here. It was jade green and fit her body snugly, with just enough dip at the neckline to show the beginning of cleavage. She quickly swooped her hair up on top of her head and secured it with combs. Glancing in the mirror, she felt excited and pretty, like she used to feel when she was going out on the town with her friends.

Her eyes glowed with excitement as she joined the three people waiting for her in the parlor.

"Oh, my!" Jack and Molly spoke in unison. Molly was the first to gain control of her voice. "Child, you are the spitting image of your—" she whispered.

"Molly!" Jack's voice cut her short, then continued, "Shannon O'Shay, you are a very beautiful young woman." Was it her imagination, or did his voice crack a little?

"We'll be back before too late," John said, taking Shannon's elbow and leading her from the house.

After they were settled in John's 4x4 Ford pickup—thankfully, a newer, more comfortable one than she'd arrived in—he turned to Shannon and said, "You really are a beautiful woman."

"Thank you," was all she could mutter.

John busied himself trying to maneuver the truck over the drying ruts in the road. The rains had stopped and the deep ruts were becoming hard and caked. It was rough going for a few minutes, but soon they were on solid ground and John leaned back in the seat to relax a little.

"John, what's going on at the Riley house? Is there some kind of mystery that I should know about? That's the second time Molly's almost said I look like someone else, but Jack stops her."

After a brief silence, as if deciding whether to tell her or not, John asked, "How much do you know about your parents' background?"

"Not much at all. When I'd try to ask questions about where they grew up, they'd always change the subject real quick, like they didn't want to talk about it."

"That's probably because they didn't," John said.

"Why? And what do you know about them?"

"Your dad grew up right here in this area. He and my dad were best friends from the time they were small boys until things fell apart for them after they were adults."

"Tell me!"

"There was also a young neighbor girl who grew up with them. Their families called them 'the Terrible Threesome.' It was kind of a joke, but some of the stories Dad's told me back up the terrible part. They were little hell-raisers. Inseparable. When you saw one, you saw the others.

"But then as they got older, both boys realized the girl was changing, and they both liked the changes. They both liked them a lot! They both fell in love with her."

"Oh, no! Trouble?" Shannon was intrigued.

"Major trouble for the Terrible Threesome. In fact, it broke the friendship up. The boys just couldn't stand the competition in that area. And eventually, your dad married the girl."

"What? The girl was my mom?"

"No. The girl was Molly."

"Are you telling me that my dad was married to Molly? I didn't know he'd been married before my mom."

"That's why they couldn't talk about their past, I guess. But, yes. He and Molly were married for five years. They had a son named Patrick."

"I have a brother?" Shock was gradually settling over Shannon.

"You had a brother. He was killed in a roping accident about eight years ago. We were branding the spring calves and he'd roped a calf and jumped off his horse to tie it up to be branded, but somehow his foot got hung in the stirrup and spooked the horse. The runaway horse dragged him to death before we could stop it. He's who you remind Molly of. He had the same red hair and green eyes as you do."

Chills covered Shannon's body as she tried to comprehend what John was telling her. She'd had an older brother all these years and never knew it. But why? Why hadn't her dad ever talked about this? Why was it such a secret?

As if hearing her silent questions, John continued, "After a few years of marriage, your dad started cheating on Molly. I'm sorry, Shannon, but your dad had a real wild streak when he was young. Anyway, as you can tell, Molly is a strong-willed woman, so even in those days when divorce was really looked down on, she left him. Her dad needed someone to take care of him anyway, so she took Patrick and went home to her dad.

"The following year, after the divorce, my dad's first cousin came back to live here on the family ranch. This ranch has been in the family for a long time. It was my great-great-grandfather's. Anyway, it didn't take long before your dad discovered she was in the area.

They'd seen each other occasionally over the years when she'd come here to visit her family. They started dating and were married within the year. She was your mom."

"You mean my mom and your dad were cousins?" This story was getting too complicated for her to keep up with.

"Yes."

"Then that makes us cousins?"

"Yes, but not that close." John said, casting her a glance.

"What do you mean?"

"Well, we're not too close kin to get married."

"Oh."

"Anyway, backing up a little, after Molly and your dad got married, my dad joined the army and went away for awhile. He met and married my mom and brought her back here. She died when I was two years old. She had some kind of kidney failure and slowly went downhill until one day, she just couldn't make it anymore. She died while Molly and your dad were still married.

"So after your parents got married, Dad started courting Molly. I don't think Dad ever stopped loving Molly, and she grew to love him, so they got married. Patrick and I grew up like brothers. I loved him very much, Shannon. I still miss him a lot."

Too overcome to speak, Shannon just sat and watched the passing scenery. Her past was wrapped around this land. She had a brother buried somewhere on this land. Her father had roamed these hills and valleys as a child. And suddenly, she knew she was home. It just felt right. She had no reason to go back to Salt Lake City. Had no desire to go back. But she had a deep hunger to find out everything she could about the story unfolding around her.

"But John, I'm confused. Why didn't Jack and Molly just tell me the truth? Why is this such a secret?"

"Shannon, you weren't really a mail order bride. You were more like a mail order bribe.

"Oh, sure, Dad and Molly would like to see me get married. And possibly to you. But that's not why you were brought here. It was supposed to look like that. And the first night when you walked in on me pitching a fit, I thought they'd brought you here for me. I knew the story, but I didn't know who you were. The next day Jack told me who you were and why you were here."

"So will you tell me?"

"Yes, but it's going to get me in deep trouble with them. But you have a right to know.

"It seems that a few months ago, your dad found a copy of an original will in your mom's things, stating that she was supposed to have inherited half of the Riley ranch. Remember, her dad and my grandfather were brothers. Well, it seems that their dad, our great-grandfather, had made a will before he died, stating that the property would be divided equally between both boys. And if, in the case of the death of one or both of them, the property would be divided equally between their heirs. Since each son only had one child, that left your mom and my dad to get the property. Our suspicion is that your mom knew about the will all the time, but, under the circum-stances, didn't want your dad to come back here and cause any trouble, so she just kept quiet about it.

"But when your dad discovered the will, he saw a chance to make some money off of it to help get his medical treatment, plus find a place for you to live after he was gone. So he wrote and told my dad that he had a choice. He could take you in and take care of you and make you an heir to the property, or your dad would force my dad to pay him the lump sum worth of half the property.

"My dad agreed to go through with it only if the secret could be kept from you until you came here and learned to love the country and the people in it. He didn't know you and was afraid that if you were like your father, you'd demand your money for your share of the ranch, and that would have been devastating for us at this time of year. We would have had to sell part of the ranch to get the money."

"So they schemed up the mail order bride story."

"Yes. Actually, it was Molly's idea. Remember, they were the Terrible Threesome. I think they actually had fun working together, scheming all this up. Almost like old times."

The flickering lights from the approaching town loomed in the distance.

"I know you have a million questions. I'll try to answer them if I can. But if you don't mind, could you let this be our secret for a while? Jack and Molly are really going to be upset with me if they know I've told you."

Shannon had a lovely evening. John turned out to be a very attentive and entertaining date. She looked at everyone in the small town with new eyes. This was her town. She felt a sense of belonging she'd never felt before. She had, indeed, come home.

The moon was full and illuminated the land with a soft blue glow as they headed back to the Riley ranch.

"I had a wonderful time, John," Shannon said, looking up at the big man beside her. She wanted to reach out and lay her hand on his arm, but didn't want to give him the wrong impression. "Thank you for tonight. But most of all, thank you for telling me who I am. I feel like I finally belong to a family. Like I have roots, somewhere. I've never felt that way before."

John pulled the truck to the side of the road.

"You *are* home, Shannon. This *is* where your roots are. This is where you belong." He took her hand in his.

The moonlight glinted on his dark brown hair, and Shannon knew he was going to kiss her. Knew it and leaned slightly toward him to encourage it.

When his lips covered hers, everything in her world fell into place. She was where she should be. In the land that was her heritage and in the arms of the man she wanted to spend her life with.

She gave herself to him in the kiss. She had to make him know that they were meant to be together. Had to make him believe that he could love again.

After a few minutes, John drew back and huskily cleared his throat. "I loved Lisa because she was petite and gave the impression that she needed someone to take care of her. She made me feel like a big man who could do anything. But when she needed me the most, I wasn't there. Late one night, the baby, a little boy, decided to come into this world early, and they both died. I was out trying to save a cow that was having a hard time giving birth to her calf. How damn ironic is that!

"It's taken me a long time to stop blaming myself. And one of the reasons is because I never got to say goodbye to her. But today, as I started my yearly celebration of getting drunk, feeling sorry for myself, and passing out, something happened. I don't know if I had a dream or saw a vision, but Lisa was in the room with me. She told me that I needed to stop mourning for her and to get on with my life.

She came to me and kissed me and told me goodbye." His voice cracked and he became quiet.

"She's right, John," Shannon said, reaching up and touching his face. "If she loved you, then you know she'd want you to be happy. And you can't be happy as long as you're in mourning about something you had no control over."

He took her hand and kissed the palm. "I loved Lisa because she made me feel like she needed me. But she never made my blood boil like you do. That's the reason I've been so nasty to you these past few weeks. You were making me feel things I never felt for her, or anyone else, and I resented you for it. Do you think we could start over? Give me a chance to get to know what a wonderful woman you are?"

"I think that would be great," Shannon said, and laid her head on his shoulder.

As the truck continued through the silvery moonlight, Shannon O'Shay remembered a long, rough ride, not long ago, and how miserable she'd been. In her wildest dreams she'd never have imagined things would turn out like this. She smiled and snuggled closer to John Riley's big, warm body, and his arm tightened around her shoulder.

She was home.

"Is he here yet?" Shannon called down the carved oak staircase.

"No, Shannon. That's the tenth time you've asked that in the past five minutes," John called up to her, pretending to be stern.

"Well, I'm anxious!" Shannon called back.

"You have to give them time to get here. The bus may not have been on time."

"I know. I know."

"They're here!" John called a little later, just as she heard the screen door squeaking open.

Shannon took one final look in the mirror. This would be the last time she'd get dressed in this room. Tonight she'd spend the night in John's bed. She adjusted the white veil and looked up as Molly walked into the room.

"You look so beautiful," Molly whispered. Tears flowed down her cheeks as she kissed Shannon.

"Thank you, Molly. You did a wonderful job on this dress. It's the most beautiful wedding dress I've ever seen."

"Go. The guests are waiting. This is the biggest wedding we've had in these parts in years."

"Did he make it?" Shannon was almost afraid to ask.

"He's here, Shannon. He doesn't look very healthy, but I think this good country air will help his condition more than anything." Molly kissed her cheek one more time and pushed her to the door.

As Shannon O'Shay walked down the staircase to her new future as Mrs. John Riley, she blessed the events that had brought her to this beautiful country. Blessed the good people who surrounded her and had insisted that her ailing dad come back to his homeland to spend his last days. Blessed the genes that gave her a body that John Riley loved.

As the piano in the parlor played and the guests turned to look at the beautiful bride, she made her way to the man she would love all the days of her life.

Dangerous Curves Ahead

www.ingramcontent.com/pod-product-compliance
Lightning Source LLC
Chambersburg PA
CBHW052145170626
46812CB00004B/1603